A QUEEN FORGED IN DEATH

THE FORGED QUEENDOM BOOK TWO

POPPY L. ROBERTS

Contents

This book is intended for adults and may contain graphic or distressing content including violence, death, and explicit sexual content.

A detailed list of content notes can be found at **authorpoppyroberts.com** if you believe something is missing from the website list please email me.

For the fairy bitches

THE QUEENDOM OF SUVIEL
GAELREST
SHARD CAVE
PASS OF SOULS
VALLEY OF ATROPIN
LAKE CLOTHO
AZURAI
TEMPLE OF HAHAOS
MT. HAVEN
NASSELLA TREE
SOUNDLESS BAY
ARACHIN
THE TWIN HARBORS
THE IDRIS
THE SINGING WOOD
DARKE MOUNTAIN
THE OAK WILDS
NIGHTSTONE PRISON
THE FATE WEAVER
SALT TEMPLE
DYING WOOD
THE ROOKERY
DRAGOS
FERNHOLME
THE TREE OF BEGINNINGS
N

Lexicon

Aduna /ah-DOO-nah/

The Goddess of Life. Aduna created all of Suviel, including the fae, and all magic comes directly from her. The elemental magics were directly gifted from her own magic during creation.

Amphipter /AM-fih-teer/

A form of legless dragon classified as a winged serpent. The females of the species are large with muted black and grey coloring while the males have brightly colored feathers and scales.

Caller

A type of kapora that acts as a lookout, sending out a loud call to any kapora in the surrounding water to alert them of danger

Fate Weaver

A mysterious entity said to be able to manipulate the threads of magic. Most likely a myth according to all texts.

Hema /HEM-ah/

A species of giant spider. They nest mainly in the mountains and are highly venomous. Most concerning, however, is the airborne hallucinogenic toxin they excrete that causes extreme rage.

Kapora /kah-POR-ah/

A small tentacled water creature with hard, horned skulls and sharp teeth. They tend to live in small bodies of water like ponds and streams, and are harmless and often helpful. They live in small schools and often surface to sunbathe but rarely leave the water.

Lachis /LAH-khiss/

Souls that are trapped on the mortal plane. They are also referred to as shades or ghosts.

Mab

The first High Queen of Suviel and the first to wield all four elements.

Mo Bhanrighit / Moh-BAN-ree-ch/

My Queen- honorific

Nassella /nah-SEL-ah/

The offspring of a voxis and fae mating pair. They have powerful glamour magic, and when their blood is used to fertilize the felbore plant, it creates a powerful drug that subdues the nassella's victims.

Necsite /NEK-sit/

Water demons, may take the shape of a horse or their natural demonic form. They most often live in deep waters and do not pose much threat to fae unless they enter their territory. The Tidal Fae are well-versed in this boundary.

Prime

The ruler of an individual court. There are four Primes in Suviel, one for each court, and all four are under the governance of the High Queen.

Salt Goddess

Minor goddess worshiped by the Tidal Fae.

Thahaos /THA-ohs/

The God of Discord, who was cast out of Suviel to become the God of Death.

The Beneath

The underworld, where the souls of the dead reside in an accord with Thahaos to maintain balance.

The Hunt

A group of wraiths selected by Thahaos to collect departed souls and ferry them to The Beneath

Voxis /VOks-is/

Wild fae who possess much of the same simple magic as the fae but are also powerful shapeshifters. The voxis are not a part of the court system but are bound by the treaty with Mab to maintain balance and self-govern.

Wraith

A deceased fae given power by Thahaos

OR

A fae-like creatures created by Thahaos in his creation of the Beneath, known as the first wraiths. They formed the original members of The Hunt.

THE QUEENDOM OF SUVIEL

HIGH COURT

Capital: Arachin

High Queen	King Consort
Lithia Caileanach	~~Narcos~~

HEARTH COURT

Capital: Fernholme   Element: Earth

Prime	Heir
Nylian	Neda

ARCANE COURT

Capital: Dragos   Element: Fire/Shadow

Prime	Heir
Astris	Calcas

CELESTIAL COURT

Capital: Galerest   Element: Air

Prime	Heir
Cassara	Halos

TIDAL COURT

Capital: Azurai   Element: Water

Prime	Heir
Osharus	Aegaea

*"Magic does not ask for belief. It
waits, patiently, beneath stone
and root, until the world
forgets, and then
it wakes."*

High Priestess Last Order of Aduna
Temple of the Unseen

CALCAS

Wake up. Wake up. **WAKE UP.**

Lithia's copper hair spilled over his arms as he cradled her limp form. *Please wake up, Lia, I just found my way back to you.* His breath burned in his chest as he swallowed the tears he refused to cry in front of Seren, or whatever Seren had become. There was a rustle of fabric as Ser knelt down at his side.

She reached down and traced a finger gently down Lithia's cheek. Cal bit down hard on the inside of his cheek, the iron taste of blood coating his tongue. Lithia was no longer hers to touch.

"She—she's gone, Cal. I can't sense her soul here any longer."

His eyes traced her features before gently laying her down and taking her voided hand in his. He followed the blackened veins where the magic had spread up her arm before unfurling across her chest, where it seized her heart. Breathing heavily, his pulse pounding behind his eyes, he turned to Seren. Quick as an asp, he dropped Lithia's hand, locked his fingers around her throat, and pulled them both to standing.

"*You* killed her."

His voice was quiet and deadly calm as Seren's eyes widened in shock. Seren gasped lightly, her hands instinctively wrapping around his wrist. His grip tightened, and while his own breath grew ragged as his rage built, hers remained even.

"Cal," she whispered.

"How?" he growled. "How did this happen? She was fine when you took me from her."

She stared at him, pity filling her honey gold eyes. "I never meant for it to go this way," Seren started, her voice cracking. "I can't control it, Cal. I never expected her to—"

The words hit him like a slap, doing nothing to soothe the storm that rose inside him. His pulse pounded in his throat. He wanted to shake her, to make her understand the weight of what she had done, what she had stolen from him, but some part of him, a small, distant part, held him back.

"You didn't mean for this to happen?" he spat his words like venom. "You used the magic. You knew what it was capable of. Its destruction is why you used it, isn't it? You've always known. You let it happen."

Her voice shook slightly. "Tell me why you care so much. I've watched you care for no one but yourself for years. Why do you care now?"

He pushed in close to her face, tightening his grip, "*No.* You tell me if Lithia's life was worth this sacrifice." His voice dropped to a low growl, each word cutting deeper. "Was *my mate* worth killing for whatever selfish plan you set into motion?"

Amusement danced through Seren's eyes, sending a frisson of fear through Cal's rage. She reached up to the place where his fingers were digging into her throat and pulled, causing him to tighten his grip. They stood in a thick silence for several minutes. Cal's raging pants began to slow as unease washed over him.

The place where his fingers met Ser's throat was warm, but something felt off. He expected her blood to be pounding under his fingers, but there wasn't even the steady thrum of a calm pulse. He concentrated for a moment, searching for the spark of life to dance under his fingertips, but there was only stillness. Dead. Of course, there was no racing pulse, no panic. Of course, she wasn't concerned. She was already fucking dead.

He threw her back as he released her throat.

"Calcas, how could I have ever expected Lia to storm in here and take on the withering curse? I promise this was not how it was supposed to happen." Seren said as she gestured towards Lia's lifeless body.

"What exactly was supposed to happen, Seren? You are killing all of Suviel, that was eventually going to include her anyway."

Seren rubbed at the skin between her brows, squeezing her eyes closed.

"Please just—just let me explain."

Cal choked on an incredulous laugh. "Do I have any other choice?"

Seren looked at him, more stoic than he remembered her ever being in life, and nodded.

"We all have choices. Let me move her body somewhere safe."

"Do not remove her fro—"

Before the protestation left his lips, there was a soft whooshing, and they were both gone. Calcas stood alone in the elaborate dining room, the silence pressing down like a lead weight. Gilded plates set with fragrant foods, and goblets filled with rich red wine. The seconds ticked by, and his anger spread through him. She had taken Lia's body from him to Thahaos only knew where.

His shadows pooled unnaturally at his feet, curling around his boots and licking their way across the floor. His knuckles whitened as he clenched his fists at his side. The flames in the braziers lining the hall began to pulse, matching the frantic rhythm of his heart.

"BRING. HER. BACK!" Cal roared at the empty room.

His shadows burst out, devouring the light in the room. The long table groaned and bowed. The gilded plates shattered, sending food flying, fruits burst and spilled to the floor in a shower of nectar and pulp. The goblets crumpled like paper, wine cascading down like blood onto the marble.

The shadows receded as Calcas crumpled to his knees, cradling his head in his hands, leaving behind shattered glass and the echoes of his fury etched into the very stones of the hall.

LITHIA

Her mouth tasted like rot.

Lithia woke slowly, a dull whooshing in her ears the only sound accompanying her racing mind. Her eyes were gritty as she tried and failed to pry them open. Pausing, she tried to feel for her body. She was lying on her back but found she could hardly move. She took a deep breath through her nose, sweet, smoky air filling her senses.

After a few moments, she tried again to open her eyes, wincing as light flooded in. She blinked hard a few times, her eyes watering as they adjusted, a warm tear rolling across her temple. Her vision was slightly blurred and tinged crimson at the edges, and she could make out nothing but uninterrupted gray.

As her vision cleared, she took in the slate gray of a cloudless sky and swaying red flowers dancing above her. She wiggled her toes and fingers and found her feeling slowly returning. She shifted, expecting a flash of pain from her void touched arm but finding none. More startling was the total lack of any soreness in her body at all. How long had she been unconscious to have been so healed?

She pulled herself to sitting and let out a hard breath as the world came into view around her. This was most certainly not the mountain temple. An iron-colored sky stretched overhead, touching the horizon on all sides, entirely uninterrupted by clouds or stars, not a ripple of light to break the monotony. In contrast, beneath it, a sea of blood red. Millions of vibrant poppies swayed on their spindly stems as far as she could see until they met the gray of the sky.

She lifted her heavy arm out towards the closest poppy. The petals were velvety and—were they warm? A chill slipped its way down her spine as the feeling of wrongness swept over her. The poppies seemed to shimmer and thrum with life. *Are they where that incessant hum is coming from?*

On the horizon, a veil of mist rolled towards her, the tendrils reaching out to her. Startled, she shifted to move but found her legs reluctant to hold her weight. Then, like a bubble meeting a blade of grass, the tension in the air popped.

"Hello, Lia dear. I never hoped to see you again so soon. I wouldn't try to stand, you haven't recouped enough strength yet."

Lia's head whipped toward the deep, layered voice as Thahaos sat in the poppies at her side.

"Ahbba?" Her voice came out in a dry croak.

The God of Death smiled down at her, his deep brown skin shifting to skeletal as he moved, handing her a waterskin.

"Drink, it will help."

She took a long sip and coughed slightly as, rather than water, something cool and sugary sweet rolled across her tongue. It was delicious. She took several more hurried sips before the layered thunder of Thahaos's laugh stopped her.

"Calm yourself, Lithia, there is more."

"Where are we?"

Thahaos continued to smile, though it no longer met his eyes. He turned away from her, looking out at the endless red. She studied his profile as they sat in silence. His features are sharp and alluring, with full lips and deep set eyes that pulse and flicker with whirls of color.

As she watched, his flesh began that shift, rich brown skin to bleached bone, subtly at first, just a flicker. Then, like the waves of a distant storm moving beneath the surface, it happened again. The smooth texture of his obsidian skin fractured into lines, revealing hints of bone, as though his body were a mere mask, a thin veil over the ancient being beneath. With a deep breath, he looked again like himself, though she supposed the skeletal version was just as much himself.

"We are in The Blooming Gate at the edge of The Beneath. This is the entrance for souls into my realm."

"Am I—" The words stuck hard in her throat.

"It appears so, only the dead can enter here unaccompanied, and I did not bring you here."

Lithia stared into the ashy sky, willing tears that would never fall. She could feel Thahaos watching her, but what do you say in the moment you wake up dead? His deep voice washed over her, the only known thing to cling to.

"I do not believe it was your time, Lia. Can you tell me what happened? The last moments you remember?"

Litha slowly told him about the time between leaving the temple and waking up in the poppies. She spent particular attention on finding the shard and the way the void clung to her body before ultimately seizing her heart. As she spoke, Thahaos stared into the distance, his eyes unfocused. The silence that followed her tale was thick.

After a few moments, he spoke. "You only attempted to take the void from the shard?"

"Yes," she replied, scrunching her nose. "That was all I could think to do in the moment, syphon out the malignant magic."

Thahaos nodded absently.

"I wonder…We said that healing all of the shards is imperative, but what if the only way to heal the part is to heal the whole? If the problem is that the shards are divided at all?"

Lithia stared at him, rolling the theory around her mind.

"So I would also need to find a way to forge the shards into a whole heart once again and then syphon the void?"

"No, my dear, I think *you are the forge*." He watched her for a breath before continuing. "I took the heart in its entirety into myself, and it broke because it was not *my* magic to hold. But it is *your* magic. If you were able to take the whole of each piece into yourself, Aduna's magic may be all it takes to heal it."

"The fairly major flaw in this plan is that I am here, and the shards are not. This sounds like a lovely theory, but I. Am. Dead."

"And as I told you before, little queen, it is not your time."

"Why do you believe that?"

"I have many reasons to believe that, the most important being that I am the God of Death, so I am usually right about these things." He smiled warmly at her. "I have sent word to someone who will be able to assess the situation on the surface and retrieve both your body and your soul."

"Who?" she asked, her voice small.

A grin split the God of Death's face.

"My daughter."

CALCAS

The silence was deafening. It pushed in on him, suffocating and thick. Cal's breath came in ragged pants as he pressed his fists into the cool stone of the floor, his knees aching from their impact with the ground as he fell. His mind tumbled in a frantic whirl, trying to grasp the thin threads tethering him to his sanity after the rage pulled him from his body. He could feel her absence like a heavy stone on his chest. Gone. Dead. *Taken.*

A shimmer disrupted the air, the scent of lemon and thyme washing over him. He snapped his head up, eyes alight with lingering fury. The air seemed to pulse for a moment.

And then, she was there.

Ser stood before him again, her opaline dress shimmering over her curves like water. Her golden eyes locked onto his, waiting. He assumed she was expecting more of his ire to wash over her.

For him to scream, demand, and rage. But he knelt in silence. His throat was tight with the grief clawing its way through his body. She had stolen Lithia's life, stolen the mate he had only just found his way back to, a mate he ran from because of *her* death, and here she stood...not dead.

A long suffering sigh escaped Seren's lips, her gaze moving to survey the room. "You're angry," she began, her voice distant and laced with something Cal couldn't quite place. " I could have controlled it, you know. The magic, the veil. All of it."

Cal stood, palming a large shard of glass, the edges biting into his palm, hot blood slipping through his fingers. "Control it? How in Thahaos's balls did you think you could control magic that destroys everything it touches? And the veil, Seren? THE VEIL? You thought you could *control* the God magic separating this realm from The Beneath? HOW?" He spat the words with a venom he had never directed at her, spit flying from his mouth.

Seren didn't so much as flinch. She watched him, calculating and steady. "You believe this to be the end, love, but it is not."

Cal flinched at the endearment. She tilted her head to the side in interest. Her eyes glazed over, seeing something far beyond him before she continued.

"There is a reason for all of this, Calcas. It all has a purpose. Lithia's death, the void." She stopped, her eyes sparkling. "You. I need you—I need your help.

He took a step back, the tension in his body unbearable. "I have spent the last decade mourning your death, Ser. I loved you. I have *just* made my way back to the path fate laid for me, and you've ripped it all away. *Again*. And now you're asking me to help you?"

"I'm not asking," she said. "I'm telling you, you'll want to help me."

"I won't be part of your madness," he said through gritted teeth.

Seren's eyes softened, and he watched the pity creeping in. "You don't understand, Cal. The realms are already crumbling. The veil is weakening, and this"—she gestured vaguely to the destruction around them—"was always inevitable. It's not just about her. It's about everything."

Cal stepped toward her again, fists clenched around the glass, voice low. "If you think I'm going to help you destroy this world, you're wrong."

For a long moment, Seren didn't speak. She merely watched him, weighing something in her mind. Then, almost as if conceding, she nodded.

"I have no choice. Neither of us does."

Before Cal could respond, before he could scream out another challenge, the air around them shimmered. A deep pull twisted within him, as though something from beyond was reaching for him, ripping him through the realm.

There was a quiet whispering sensation, like fingers brushing against his mind, urging him to *listen*, to *understand*. Then there was nothing but blinding light as his eyes focused.

Blinking, Cal took in the growing decay in front of him. The void encroached on the land like a shadow, leaving nothing but ash in its wake. The once prospering fields on the southern tip of Suviel were blackened and barren.

"It's already too late," Seren whispered, her voice barely audible over the pulse in his ears. "The realms are collapsing in on one another. The world is dying. And the only way to fix it—to *save* it—is to shatter the veil. Once it's gone, everything will be...restored. Cal, it will all be together. *We will all be together.*"

His heart hammered in his chest. His instincts screamed at him to run, to push her away, to reject everything she was saying. But the reality of what she was offering, the burden in her voice, made him wait, tumbling the possibilities around in his mind, smoothing its rough edges like stones in rushing water. He watched in silence as the wind stirred the ashes at his feet, sending them skittering across the dry ground.

"I'm not asking for forgiveness," Seren said quietly, her hand reaching out. "I'm asking for trust."

It was the smallest gesture. A hand extended in the darkness, a plea that Calcas stared down, the pain in his chest bellowing to be heard.

His mind told him that there were other options and that this was not the answer. But his heart...*his heart knew* that if he didn't follow her now, if he didn't trust her *this one last time,* the world he loved...the mate he loved, would both cease to exist. The idea itself felt like a betrayal of every belief he had ever held.

With a jagged breath, he stepped forward and took her hand.

They ate in an odd silence at the still destroyed table. Someone had laid out a simpler meal while they were gone, but Calcas didn't have the energy to ask any clarifying questions. The silence was filled with the soft sounds of clinking cutlery and the weight of unspoken truths. Cal's mind churned at the rapid way information had come at him in the last few days.

Cal could feel the coldness of his anger encasing his heart, but beneath it, there was something else—something older, a flicker of grief, a trace of the love he had once felt for Seren. It was all tangled up with sorrow and rage, and he didn't know how to untwine the treads. Not yet. Maybe never.

This new version of Seren seemed at odds with the Seren that took up that corner of his mind. This Seren sat across from him, unreadable. She hadn't flinched, she had accepted the storm of his fury with that cold calm that stood in opposition to the fiery love he remembered. But now, as he sat there, he couldn't decide if it was the calm that haunted him or the absence of her warmth.

"I never told you how I found out Lithia was my mate," Cal said, the words tumbling from his lips like they'd been waiting too long to be said.

LITHIA

Lithia stared at the God of Death lounging calmly in the endless red of The Blooming Gate. His eyes were closed, face tipped up to where she assumed a sun would be in the infinite bleakness of the sky. She had been dead for three days, or that's what she assumed based on the three dinners she had shared with Thahaos. There wasn't much else to use as a marker, no light changes in the sky, no sleep, only endless red and gray. She assumed there would be a point where you just stayed dead, and three days seemed well past that marker, but she couldn't make herself ask.

"Staring at me isn't practicing, little queen."

Lithia narrowed her eyes at the smirk tugging at the corner of Thahaos's lips. She then looked just beyond him to the swath of blackened, wilted poppies. Her first attempt to focus her syphon had been comically bad. She had ripped the life and color from an entire section of the poppy field, rendering it lifeless. She had spent nearly the whole of her time here quietly practicing, taking the quiet corrections from Thahaos.

She had made enormous progress, but quietly she knew that the peaceful environment, free of any distractions but her thoughts, was likely a major factor in that. She looked down at the wilted collection of flowers in front of her and breathed in deeply; Thahaos's layered voice washed over her once more.

"Focus on the magic, not its life. You don't want its life, only its spark."

She closed her eyes as she breathed, pushing down the tempest in her mind that threatened to rise in the silence. Slowly, she opened her eyes, focusing on the single stem in front of her, swaying in some phantom wind she couldn't feel. She let out the tendrils of her magic, slowly feeling for the ashy floral scent of its magical core. Plucking through the simple threads of its life, she curled her magic around the single bitter ash thread amongst the overpowering floral tang. Tenderly, she pulled, letting the acrid magic wash across her tongue. It took enormous effort, but at the first hint of spicy floral, she stopped and released the now dead thread of magic.

Panting slightly, she blinked several times at the poppy in front of her. It was still standing, still swaying in the wind, but all its color was gone. She reached out and touched a velvety gray petal, feeling life still humming through it. She looked up sharply, a grin spreading on her face, to find Thahaos watching her, a blinding smile splitting his usually reserved features. Lithia's smile turned sly.

"Does this mean you'll tell me who your daughter is now?"

Thahaos let out a laugh that vibrated like thunder through her bones. "No, I think I'll hold that secret until she arrives, little queen."

Lithia feigned a scowl. They had been having this exact conversation multiple times a day, and he wouldn't budge. She had a bone deep feeling of who she was and just wanted the confirmation.

"I am so proud of you, Lia. You have done well."

She let out a heavy breath at the feeling of parental affirmation she desperately missed. Her mind began its spiral into the tormented grief plaguing her.

"Tell me again about what happened when you found the shard?" Thahaos's quiet question pulled her back from the brink.

Lithia blinked hard a few times to clear the burning behind her eyes. It was beginning to feel like lifetimes separated her from her death, not mere days. She nodded slowly, her eyes glazing slightly as she pulled up the memories, running her hands through the lush grass.

"I am missing quite a bit of time, of course, from when I collapsed after touching the shard to waking in the cells. We—"

She choked slightly. "We were talking in the cells when an armored male appeared out of nowhere and dragged Cal from his cell."

She was getting rather tired of telling him the story. He seemed to be trying to glean information from it, but hadn't gotten any further than before. With a sigh, she continued.

"Then another fae in that same strange armor appeared—"

Thahaos interrupted her, his head cocked to the side. "Did you not recognize the armor?"

A wrinkle formed between her brows. "No, it wasn't like any armor I've seen before. Polished silver set with opaline. The crest was equally unfamiliar, swords and a crowned helm."

She watched as Thahaos's eyes narrowed at her words, and she sat in silence, not wanting to interrupt the thoughts she could see rolling like storm clouds behind his eyes.

"You recognized none of these fae?"

Lithia sat for a moment, confused. Why would she recognize them?

"No, of course not."

A crack of thunder rolled across the sky, and Thahaos was gone. She looked around the clearing in alarm, but before the thunder faded, he was back, standing before her. His features flickered quickly between the rich ebony of his skin and his skeletal form, a large piece of aged wood clenched in his hand. He looked at her for a few silent breaths, his expression darkening. Slowly, with a slight hesitation, he passed her the slab.

Her nose wrinkled slightly at the sudden change in demeanor as she took the worn wood in her hands. The breath caught in her chest as she turned it over, finding glimmering opaline pressed into the soft wood. Two swords crossed beneath a crowned helm. Lithia blinked down at the crest several times, the questions forming a dam in her throat, a prickle of unease creeping up her spine.

"How..."

They stared at each other in tense silence for several minutes. Finally, he spoke, his voice low and weighed down by the same unknown emotion clouding his eyes.

"It is one of mine."

"Yours?" she echoed, the word tasting wrong on her tongue. Lia stood slowly, feeling like the ground was spinning below her.

Thahaos nodded, smoke swirling in his eyes. "Wraiths. There are several houses here, just as there are in Suveil. Most are headed by the first wraiths, those I created in the beginning. Those that I believe you saw, however, would be The Hunt. I did not summon them, nor did I assign them this task. I called for them, but have not received an answer so far. Their armor, though, is distinct, so I am sure this is who you encountered."

"I don't understand."

"Truthfully, little queen, I do not understand myself. While they do follow my orders, they are also very much capable of free will."

"What would they want with me? Are they the ones who cursed the shard? What could they possibly gain in that?"

"I fear that is nothing either of us can answer from here."

Lithia's shoulders curled inward. She was failing yet again. Suviel needed her to be working to figure anything out, and she was sitting in a field of flowers, chatting with a God. *Dead*.

"You are not to blame for your current situation, Lithia. You will be free of this place, and you will save your people. Do not give up on yourself when your journey hasn't even begun."

She looked up into the face of the God of Death and found a small, sad smile on his face. He reached out a hand towards her.

"Come, little queen, let me show you The Beneath."

The world blurred around them as she took his hand.

Calcas

Ser didn't speak, but her eyes narrowed, her posture going rigid, bracing herself. Cal could feel the shift in the air. She wanted to know, but didn't like having lost control of the conversation.

"Several years before the battle in the Valley of Atropin, I felt the first stirrings of a mate bond. It felt like a vine growing its way into my magical core, slipping between the threads of magic." Cal sat back in his chair with a low sigh. "I was so hopelessly in love with you that day...I assumed it was you."

Seren's brow wrinkled slightly, a flicker of confusion breaking through her closed expression. He cleared his throat before continuing.

"We were meeting in Arachin because of the voxis attacks, and it tugged when you walked into the throne room. I was a bit too single minded to realize that Lia was right beside you." He paused and huffed a laugh. "To be honest, I think I could have convinced myself it was you if you had been on the other side of the queendom each time I felt anything."

His smile was small as his gaze slid out of focus.

Ser coughed quietly. "And when did you realize it wasn't?"

"One night, we were waiting for a report from you and Wil. You were on some scouting trip in the mountains, and I was mad at her for sending you and she—I knew and I panicked."

Cal reached forward and downed his wine, refilling it and draining it once more before continuing.

"So I found a fate weaver—"

"You did *WHAT*?"

"I didn't say it was a particularly good choice, Seren." She flinched slightly at the use of her full name, but he continued. "There is one who lives near Dragos, and I was headed home anyway."

"You tried to get her to sever your mate bond?"

"Them, and no? I don't know if that was my intention originally. I was confused. I asked if they would help me figure out who my mate was and tell me what to do if I loved someone else. What they ended up telling me was 'the one I love wasn't the one fate chose, but fate chose the one I love,' and I almost ripped their throat out."

Ser leaned forward as he spoke, brow furrowed.

Cal sighed. He had asked the fate weaver an embarrassing number of questions, but the feeling of loss and confusion sitting in their humid cottage had been overwhelming. They seemed to take some pity on him and offered to unweave his fate, severing the mate bond with Lia. The idea was tempting for only a fleeting moment. He couldn't risk his magic, but more than that, he wouldn't risk Lithia's.

Now, Cal looked into Seren's eyes for any spark of her former warmth before he continued and found none. He realized for the first time that he had been choosing Lithia ever since that day in a million different nonromantic ways, and he almost laughed. Just hours ago, he told Lia that it was a blessing that the bond didn't make you choose, that it can't make you love, but he had been choosing her all along. Now here he was, a breath into loving her, and she was gone.

"The weaver offered to sever my bond, but I declined." He clipped the sentence, reaching again for his wine.

Ser narrowed her eyes at him. "Why?"

"Why? I didn't want some crone digging around in my fate threads, Seren. What if she snipped the wrong one?" He plastered a half-assed smirk on his face.

"If you didn't go through with having the bond severed, why did you never tell either of us? Why did you run from her like a wounded animal after Atropin?"

Cal shrugged, raking his hand through his hair. "I didn't tell you because my research into mate bonds said that they can't force you to love, so I assumed we could just go on as we were. As for the other part," the mask he was wrestling into place slipped slightly, "I left her because I blamed her for your death, and feeling my magic pull toward her felt like that spear driving into my chest anew every time."

Ser stared at him for several long seconds, and he cut her off before she could ask her more questions.

"Now, I've told you a story, so it's time you tell me one. What the hell are you doing, Seren?"

Seren leaned forward on her elbows, steepling her fingers beneath her chin.

"The last thing I saw with my living eyes was Lia's gore streaked face looking down at me, surrounded by a bright blue sky. I could hear her begging me not to leave her. My own words were blood in my throat, and all I wanted was to tell her I loved her one more time before the darkness swallowed me whole. It took all my energy, and it burned like fire. I could see the blood from my breath landing on her cheek, but I did it. I told her, I promised her, that I loved her in this life and the next. Then death swallowed me."

Cal's heart ached, and pressure built behind his eyes, but he stayed still and silent, not wanting her to stop talking.

"When I opened my eyes again, Thahaos was there, offering me this."

She held out her hand, and in it materialized the gleaming silver crowned helm she had worn earlier when she revealed herself to him.

"He invited me to lead The Hunt, to become a wraith, roaming the land of the living, guiding the fleeing souls into The Beneath. I had opened my eyes on my next life, and I still loved her." She looked up at him, searching his face. "Still loved you."

Cal remained frozen, unwilling to react.

She smiled sadly. "I took the helm, I led The Hunt, and I watched. I watched you both living and moving further and further and further apart. I could see so much pain, and I was in so much pain. About a year of your time, after Atropin, I started looking for a way to just speak to you again. It was driving me mad that I could see you, but I couldn't interact with you at all."

Seren blew out a long breath. "Thahaos realized what I was searching for and he is a kind God, he explained that few could cross the veil in such a way, and those who had once been alive were not permitted to do so. The veil is what was keeping me from you both, so I decided that I would find a way through it. At first, the idea was really just to find a rift, a way through, but the more I spoke with the others and the more pain I saw, I realized it was more than just me."

She leaned forward eagerly, and Cal found himself leaning into her, hanging on her words, searching for something redeemable.

"The veil was created to punish Thahaos, and in turn, it punished the fae as well. Thahaos is the one who brought death to Suviel; it is a result of his greed. If we found a way to shatter the veil, to free Thahaos from this prison of the Gods, making The Beneath would become a part of Suviel. The dead who have been restored in The Beneath would once again be able to walk among the living in Suviel."

Cal sat back in his seat, her words spinning in his mind. If she were successful, he would have Lia again, and not just her, so many others would once again be restored.

"But the magic is actively killing the fae at this pace, all of Suviel will be in The Beneath soon anyway, and Suviel itself will be a wasteland."

Ser nodded, chewing her lip. "The spell is...incomplete."

He scrubbed the heels of his hands into his eyes. "What do you mean, incomplete, Seren?"

"It was working, that's why I'm standing here, able to be seen and touched by you. But the wraith who cast it died before he finished, that's why the creatures are losing their higher functions and the land is dying, it's leaching magic to feed the spell. That's why I need your help."

"What in the Goddess's tits makes you think I can cast a spell, Ser?"

"Not you, Calcas," she said with no small amount of annoyance. "I need you to convince Willow to help us."

"Why do you think she can do what you need? No. Why do you think she'll do anything I ask?"

"She cares for you more than any other fae, Calcas. You are her chosen family, she will help if you ask, and I know she is able to do what I need. You know very well that she is powerful."

"Yes, bu—"

"She can do it, Cal, please. I just—I want Lia back. I want you both back."

LITHIA

They walked through the poppies, Lia peppering Thahaos with questions about his realm. The poppies were just the entrance, where souls landed until they were ready to move on, further into The Beneath. He told her some would stay in The Blooming Gate for ages, waiting for another soul to join them. The soul is the only one who knows when it is ready to move on from that place, so some never leave, while some never fully stop before passing through.

As they crested a hill, a chasm came into view, the first change in landscape since she opened her eyes. On the other side, she could make out the shape of buildings. It was like looking across the bay at the Twin Harbors on a foggy night.

"Welcome to my home, little queen. The city of Odux."

"There's a whole city?"

"You didn't expect me to live in a cave, did you?" Thahaos laughed, rich and melodic. "Yes, there is a city, there are no courts, but there is a hierarchy. My wraiths, the ones I created in the beginning, manage different wards of the city. Then The Hunt, made up of the most honorable dead, or so I believed."

He shook his head and turned, walking along the edge of the chasm. Lia stopped staring out at the distant world she was about to enter.

"Is my—Are my parents there? Is Nars?"

"Ahh, Narcos is not there. His soul is in the poppies, very near where you sat. Though I expect he awaits his twin. As for your mother, she is not here at all. When she died, she was taken by Aduna, as were the queens before her, as you should have been. I suspect the fracture in your magic has harmed that connection. You are the first queen to ever walk The Beneath," He bowed low, "and I am honored, Mo Bhanrighit."

Lia swallowed thickly. "My father?"

Thahaos smiled softly. "Yes, little queen, he is here. I can take you to see him. You won't be able to speak with the souls here though. You have not passed on fully."

"Please, anything is enough."

They continued walking for a short time until a low bridge came into view. It wasn't grand or ornate, simple wood spanning the maw of the chasm. Thahaos held out his arm and she slipped her hand into the crook of his elbow as they crossed the expense.

She moved slightly to look over the side into the chasm but felt a slight pull on her hand.

"Do not. This is where the souls who do not deserve rest go. There is nothing but misery to see beneath the mist."

She tucked herself in closer to the God at her side and shuddered in relief as they stepped onto the soft grass on the other side. The white stone buildings reminded her of the port towns in the Tidal Court, though with an obvious lack of the blistering sun and simmering teal water.

They wandered through neat, cobbled streets for over an hour. Lithia was so enraptured that she nearly forgot that she was, in fact, in The Beneath. None of the fae around them seemed to be able to see them because they maneuvered their way entirely uninterrupted.

Soon, they passed through a small square with a sea glass tiled fountain before pushing through a large arched gateway. Lithia was about to turn to ask where they were when her breath caught in her throat. A male dressed in green linen sat on a large woven rug, telling an animated story to a group of younglings. A male with a scruffy beard, deep green eyes, and curly copper hair shot through with gold.

Her father looked exactly as lively and kind as she remembered. Cillian had died when Lia was 112 years old in a hunting accident. She was so angry with her mother because he hated to hunt, but her mother had insisted they needed to keep up their friendships with the Prime families, so he went.

Thahaos's deep voice rolled into her thoughts, *"Do you hear the story he's telling?"*

She paused and listened, letting the sound of his voice wash over her. Then she laughed. He was telling these children a story about her. It was one of the numerous times she and Calcas had gotten caught doing something reckless as younglings because they were constantly trying to be the most daring, the strongest.

"Who are these children?"

Thahaos's smile grew sad. "They are the ones whose families haven't joined them. Children tend not to linger in the poppies."

"Your father is a kind man. His soul did not linger in the poppies. He knew you and your mother would never join him, and instead, he gives his love to the children, and he is loved deeply in return."

"Thank you," she choked out through her tears, taking one more look at her father before leaving the way they came.

Thahaos came up beside her and took her hand in his. "Your fate is unkind, little queen, and I am so sorry. I hope that when you have healed this magic, you can change your fate."

He leaned down and kissed her on the forehead, and when she opened her eyes, they were back in The Blooming Gate.

Lia sat down, looking at the single gray poppy she had syphoned the magic from, and wept. She cried for her father, for

Narcos, whose soul was separated from its twin, for Tadhg, for Suviel, but mostly, selfishly, she cried for herself. She cried for the deep sense of failure that seemed to follow her like a curse. For the fate that had carved itself onto her bones. She cried until there was nothing left. Then she stared down into the poppies and began to feel for the threads of magic, searching for the ashy thread, and slowly she began to syphon.

Calcas

Cal stared into the odd swirling nebula that was the Celestial Shard and watched the void of magic slip around like oil on water, unnatural, like you could easily wipe it off. It was a smudge on the magic, an ink stain on paper, and it had taken down his queen, his general, his longest friend, his mate. He tore his eyes from the magic and turned towards the swirling path that led deeper into the hidden garden.

He followed the winding flagstone until he came upon the glittering crystal clear lagoon surrounded, inexplicably, by floating trees. He sank down on a soft patch of grass near the edge of the water and lay back with his eyes screwed shut, wondering where he made the choices that led them here. He opened his eyes and found himself staring up into the roots of a large tree that had drifted his way.

He followed the twisting roots, tracing their intricate patterns, thinking he could stay here and sink into the soil and no one would ever find him. He wouldn't have to figure out Seren's true motives. He wouldn't have to face his queendom with the news that Lia was dead. He wouldn't have to look into the knowing white of Wil's eyes and tell her he failed so completely.

He shimmied himself clear of the floating roots and stood slowly, surveying the night garden around him. He followed the gently curling path, brushing his fingers on the velvet soft pink and purple leaves lining the walkway. The path curved outward, leading him back toward a reality he had no desire to face but no way of escaping.

Cal came to a stop in front of the small carved doorway that would lead him out of this hidden temple. A simple frame that separated him from nonexistence and the flaming face of his failure, and he had no choice but to step through it.

The sunlight bathed the Valley of Atropin in gold. Cal stared at its glittering beauty from the entrance to the Pass of Souls. He knew in a few hours that simmering gold would turn molten, burning those within to ash with the failure he had clogging his throat.

He compulsively gripped and released the hilt of the dragon glass sword at his waist and started moving towards the line of crumbling homes near the lake in the distance.

It was midday when he came level with the first building, or the crumbling remains of what used to be a home. A shadow moved overhead, and he looked up into the sun and found the amphiptere from Thahaos's temple circling above.

"Othis?"

He let out a deafening screech before spiraling towards Cal. He froze, panicked, for a heartbeat before the massive creature landed with a thunderous boom on the packed dirt road before him, laying his head down, bringing him face to...snout with Cal.

Cal and Othis stared at each other for several minutes. Was Miana or Thahaos trying to reach him? Was Othis trying to tell him something? What in the Goddess's tits was happening? He kept waiting for anything to happen, but Othis just...watched, steam silently curling from each nostril with each huff of breath.

After several minutes, Cal slowly reached out a hand and placed his palm flat on the smooth scales of Othis's face. Heat radiated from the deep purple scales, and the amphiptere nuzzled into his touch.

"He normally doesn't let males touch him, but his liking you *and* Tadhg is just ridiculous."

Cal's shoulders snapped to attention at the low silk of Wil's voice. He stepped to the side to find Wil running her hand down one feathered wing as she watched him. Just past them, he could see Neda and Tadhg finally coming up level with Othis, Neda walking in a large arc to avoid him and Tadhg skipping right up and scratching at a spot just behind the amphiptere's wing joint, causing it to flop to the side, exposing its belly, which Tadhg promptly began to scratch with both hands.

Cal stared slightly dumbfounded at the sight.

"May as well close your mouth, the big baby loves him for some reason," Neda said with a frown.

"Ignore her, she's mad because he hates her."

He watched the happy banter, knowing that the first words out of his mouth were about to crush it all. He inhaled deeply through his nose, the ash and brimstone scent of Othis mixing with the sweet new growth smell of the valley.

"Lia—"

Wil cut him off, "We know Cal."

The words that had been attempting to choke him died in a breath on his tongue. He looked between the three, Neda had deep purple circles under both eyes, the lines in Wil's brow seemed to have etched themselves deeper, and Tadhg—the usually inexplicably happy fae's shoulders were hunched forward, and he had yet to look at Cal at all.

"How do you know? Did Ser tell—"

"SER?"

"Seren?"

Tadhg's head snapped in his direction, Wil and Neda's voices overlapping in confusion. Cal looked at their panicked faces and shook his head to clear the tide of questions now threatening to pull him under.

"Not here," Wil said, her white eyes narrowed on Cal.

She turned sharply on her heel and, hooking her arm through Neda's, dragged them both back towards the fortified ruin they had commandeered as a base.

Tadhg fell in step beside him as he passed, and they walked in silence down the hard packed street. As they reached the crumbling steps, Tadhg's hand fell heavy on his shoulder haunting him in his tracks.

"No one thinks you failed, Cal. I'm sure you believe it of yourself but remember you aren't walking into a room filled with your enemies. None of our shoulders are light."

He turned to the healer and stared into his violet eyes, finding nothing but concern and acceptance shimmering in their depths. He nodded curtly before reaching out and pulling Tadhg to him. The healer quickly returned the embrace. When he pulled back, Cal found an impish grin splitting his face.

"Ah, I knew you secretly liked me, you big brute, don't worry, I won't tell."

Cal pushed him up the stairs with a small shake of his head. He followed Tadhg's swinging white braids down the threadbare hall towards the still standing ornate doors at the end. They slipped through into a severely neglected library. The deep wood table that dominated the center of the room looked out of place, like it was pilfered from another room or home entirely. Its dark surface was covered in the maps, books, and notes that he and Lia had sent ahead of them.

At the far end of the table was Aegaea, twirling her deep red hair around a pale finger, her bare feet crossed on the tabletop. Seafoam green eyes flitted his direction, widening slightly as they locked on his. She nodded to him before returning her gaze to the damp looking tome resting on her lap.

Each of them pulled out mismatched chairs and sank down at the table, the silence thickening with each moment. Cal pulled a worn armchair up to the table, divesting himself of his armor before perching on the edge of his seat.

Wil leaned forward on the table, lacing her fingers together, and stared at Cal. He swallowed a bracing breath before he crumbled everything.

CALCAS

The entire group was leaning into his story, even Aegaea had shifted from her relaxed posture to rapt attention at some point, dropping her book with a wet thump.

When he finally caught up to meet them in the valley, the silence resettled around them. Cal could feel the questions rattling, charging the air around them, ready to explode. As usual, Tadhg was the first to catch up, his mind running far faster than anyone else Cal had ever encountered.

"Seren is...*alive?*"

"No," he and Wil asserted in unison.

Tadhg looked between them, waiting for one of them to explain, but neither did. Instead, Cal leaned toward Wil's penetrating stare.

"You said you already knew about Lia. If you didn't know because of Seren, then how?"

Wil reached into a pocket on her vest and pulled out a folded piece of parchment, sliding it across the table to him. From the corner of his eye, he saw Neda and Tadhg share a look as he picked it up, unfolded it, and read the short note written in elegant script.

Willow,

Lithia's soul has arrived in The Beneath, something is wrong, it is not her time.

Ahbba

He read it several times, a wrinkle forming between his brows.

"Thahaos told you? I guess that makes sense, we had just been with him."

Something was itching the back of his mind as he read the note again, then it slid into place, and he jerked his gaze up to meet Wil's so quickly his muscles protested. Deep black skin, purple hair, white eyes... *"Kill me, wraith."*

"Tadhg said I looked so much like my mother that it was an impossible likeness to miss."

Tadhg nodded. "If Miana's hair wasn't more white than purple, you could be twins."

Willow's smile was small. "I expect mine will match hers one day yet."

"You—you are the daughter of a God?"

Wil nodded. "I was born in the temple during the reign of Lia's great-grandmother, Ilena, 2157 years ago."

Cal felt a collective intake of breath. It seems that everyone knew she was Thahaos's daughter, but no one expected her to tell her story.

"I grew up with my mother on the path to becoming a priestess, taking care of the temple, and learning to control my power. It was a rather mundane existence, to be honest. I didn't leave the temple for my first 700 years or so of life; there was no need. As I grew, however, I realized I wanted more than to just exist within those walls, so I trained. I trained in combat, in stealth, I read every book, tome, and scroll in that great library, I honed my power into a lethal weapon, and I learned everything I could about the outside world through the crows."

"I prayed over the souls with my father every time he visited. I begged him to take me with him when he left. He always said my place was with my mother, and he left me behind. Thahaos is the God of the dead, so obviously, I spent a significant amount of time honoring the dead, and any priestess does. The biggest difference between The Temple of the Beneath and the temples to most other Gods is that we have active work to do."

Tadhg slid a cup of tea in front of Cal. He hadn't heard anyone move or leave, but he nodded his thanks before turning his focus back to Wil as she continued.

"For nearly 400 years, I helped to ferry the souls from their death to the poppy fields where they stay before they pass through the gates of judgment. You heard that voxis and the nassella call me 'wraith' before their deaths because that is what I am. I do not ferry the dead any longer, but I am a wraith. I am not just a wraith, though. My mother is a wraith, the High Priestess of the Temple of Thahaos, but my father is a God, which makes me something entirely new, an unknown. I am a Godling, the only Godling."

Cal could feel that his face had gone slightly slack jawed the longer she spoke.

"So you're like really old."

They all turned to Tadhg, and Wil started to laugh. After a few moments, Tadhg began to laugh as well, and it spread like a contagion through the room, with Neda and Aegaea joining in. It was infectious, and eventually Cal felt himself rumbling with quiet laughter as well. Their laughter slowed, Wil wiped a tear from her face.

"I can't believe that's the part of the story that stuck with you."

He sobered slightly and fidgeted in his seat, his eyes darting to Cal and Neda.

"Well, since we are being honest. I figured out who you were decades ago, so I've always known. I mean, it's not like the resemblance isn't there. I met you for the first time only months after I left the temple, so it just clicked."

Wil smiled softly at him. "Thank you for your silence, Tadhg."

He nodded reverently.

"Why have you never told us?" Neda asked, the layer of hurt in her question deeper than Cal expected.

Wil tilted her head.

"Cal, do you remember when you and Lia first joined the Legion? She wanted to go through training without anyone knowing who you both were to prove you got only what you earned." He nodded, the understanding sinking like a stone in his gut. "I very much doubt we would be the friends we are had my parentage been known. It has been the greatest freedom to exist outside those bonds for so long. The time has come, though."

Neda nodded absently, her eyes glazed. "So you always knew so much because—"

"Because I have seen much."

Cal cleared his throat. "Thank you for trusting us."

Wil bowed her head to them.

"You followed Lia into all of this knowing this was the outcome." Aegaea's sing-song voice broke in for the first time. She reached out and took Wil's hand in hers. "That is a great sacrifice, Willow, Daughter of Thahaos, one we should not waste."

CALCAS

Night had fallen thick and dark. The lachis, spirits trapped in the valley, had awoken with the nightfall, and their anguish was audible in the stillness. Moans and shrieking filled the darkness, a valley of despair, so much of it at his own hands.

Wil sank into the chair beside him and stared into the darkness, silent for several minutes.

"Cal, I know you want to believe that Seren's intentions are good, but I do not believe any good will come from this plan. She was appointed to The Hunt immediately upon her death because of who she was in life. This is not the normal path. Souls normally move through The Beneath like normal and reside there for generations before being given such an honor. I fear her connection to life was too strong, and it poisoned her mind."

"I know, and she isn't Ser. She was cold and calculating in a way she never was in life. I'm confused and raw, and I just can't piece together what she was thinking when she made this plan. It's madness. She can't have truly believed any good was going to come from it."

"It is possible she is hiding her true motives from you to draw your heart to her cause, especially if she believes she needs me to help her. I do not believe her motives are good, but more importantly," she leaned forward, her eyes locked on some distance far over Lake Clotho, "I do not believe the world she has painted is possible."

Cal stared at her profile. He took in all the small pieces of Willow that always made her seem...more. Her eyes weren't just white, they swirled like smoke in a looking glass, as if he looked deep enough, he would simply fall through into their depths. Her features we regal, dark arched brows, full lips, and delicately pointed ears, all wrapped in the feathered armor she always wore.

Her connection to the crows and her predatory aura were the most telling attributes of her station. He marveled at how he had lived a life alongside her for so long and missed it all. She was a marvel, and he was immeasurably unworthy of her friendship, and yet she had given it freely for so long.

"I don't know if I can just not try, Wil. I'm—" He took a shuddering breath, his throat burning. "I'm not strong enough to lose them both."

"You aren't losing them both, Cal, you saw Ahbba's note, we are going to get Lia. You and I...and Othis," she said with a small smile.

He didn't return it, and she sighed, leaning her head back on her chair. They sat in silence, listening to the wailing of the souls in the valley.

"I still love her, Wil."

"I know."

"So what's your plan for Lia?"

Neda rolled her eyes as Cal plopped down at the table beside her. "Well, our plan was mainly guesswork before because we had no idea where your bodies were. Wil can retrieve Lia's soul, but she needs to be able to reunite it with her body. With your bounding back in with, arguably the most absurd story I've ever heard, we should be able to formulate a real plan for Wil to get her."

"For me and Wil to get her."

"I highly doubt Wil needs—"

"He is coming, Neda."

Neda huffed and bit aggressively into the piece of ham in her hand, grumbling under her breath as she chewed. Wil moved the rest of the way into the cluttered library, taking up her seat across from them and smiling at Neda's theatrics. If Cal were to guess, there had been several heated discussions about how it would be easier if Wil went to retrieve Lia alone before he arrived.

"We need to make a plan quickly and go as soon as possible. I don't want her to linger, and I don't want to allow the void to spread while we plot."

Cal and Neda mutter agreements in unison. Tadhg bounded into the library and nodded good morning to each of them sitting beside Wil and turning to her fully as he spoke.

"Aegaea is retrieving a few more texts from her mother's library. She will return quickly, but likely not before you leave. She believes she has figured out where the Tidal magic is, but she sounded concerned."

"Did she say?"

"No, she jumped into the lake mid-sentence like always," he said on a laugh. "I also called for Othis, he should be here soon."

"Thank you." Wil turned back to Neda and Cal. "We should make a plan before he arrives so we can leave quickly. Truthfully, gathering her soul from The Beneath should be the easier part. Ahbba will hold her soul in The Blooming Gate, and it is a journey I have made many times. Though admittedly, never with a living passenger. Cal, tell me about where her body is again."

Cal recounted in as much detail as he could the hidden mountain sanctuary that housed the Celestial Shard. His eyes rimmed in silver as he finished. "Wil, I don't know where in that labyrinth her body is. Ser took her after she died; she could be anywhere."

"That is still a much smaller area than we were originally going to have to search. The larger issue is The Hunt. If they fight…"

"If they think we are there to help? They are expecting us."

"They are expecting us. Not Lia."

Cal nodded absently.

Neda sighed. "Wil, are you able to conceal Lia's soul from them?"

Wil tilted her head to the side slightly. "Yes, in theory, or Ahbba could cloak it."

"Then you only need to get out. You have a way in, and you even have a way to find her body. You only need a way out. There are too many unknowns. You are going to have to plan your exit once you have her."

"That's reckless," Wil said, her eyes locked tight with Neda's.

Neda shrugged. "You have half a map, so you can make half a plan."

Wil stood quickly, leaning over the table, fists pressing into the tabletop, splitting the rotting wood beneath her knuckles.

"You do not get to act like a petula—"

An ear-splitting screech tore through her anger, shaking the windows in their panes. A shadow passed the window a split second before the floor rocked with the weight of Othis landing outside.

Cal stood, pushing his chair back from the table with some force.

"It doesn't matter, it's time to go get our queen."

Wil kicked the chair from behind her and stomped from the room. Cal followed slowly behind her, aiming for his small room. He closed the door quietly behind himself, letting out a harsh breath before padding across the mildewed rug and beginning to pull on his weapons, strapping them across his body soundly and belting Lia's sword at his waist.

He lingered in the doorframe for several minutes before trudging down the hall towards the doors he had just entered, though only the afternoon before. He heard quiet arguing coming from a door near the end of the hall as he approached. Stealing a quiet glance inside, he saw the rushed moment Neda pulled Wil into her, kissing her fiercely, and smiled to himself, slipping quietly past and out into the bright sunlight.

He found Tadhg feeding large fish to Othis, who was curled contentedly in the weeds beside the crumbling home. Nestled between the large creature's wing joints was a long double saddle, similar to the ones the riders in his court used on their bonded amphiptere. This one, however, was longer and narrower without any of the saddlebags and bulk he was accustomed to seeing. This one was not meant to carry anything but its riders.

He ran his palm down the warm scales of Othis's long neck until he reached the saddle straps. He pressed his forehead to the smooth scales and let the calm, even breathing steady his own. He stayed there even as he heard the approach of intentional footsteps come to a stop beside him.

"Come, Cal, death is only the first stop."

He stepped back as Othis leaned towards them, allowing Wil to pull herself into the saddle. Cal stood still, staring at the half of the saddle he was evidently meant to sit on, but couldn't make himself move. Othis chuffed a stream of smoke and flicked his tail towards Cal's feet. Wil held a hand out and Cal stepped forward, gripping her hand and nestling his foot in the wing joint where he had seen Wil step, and threw his leg up and over the saddle just like he would Redmaw's. He settled in behind Wil, his thighs tightening on the serpentine body beneath him.

Othis straightened and shook his wings out, sending a ripple through his body and making Cal's stomach lurch. Grabbing hold of the horn in front of him, he expected to see Wil taking up some sort of reins and was confused to find her sitting calmly holding a horn as well.

"Where are his reins?"

Othis huffed out another billow of smoke as he spread his wings wide beneath them.

"He wouldn't listen to me even if he had reins," Wil laughed. "He knows where he is going."

With a mighty screech and a single powerful pump of his wings, Othis launched them into the clouds.

LITHIA

Lia sat alone in the poppies, tears streaming down her cheeks. She cried and she poured herself out in a never-ending deluge. She told story after story, she sent an endless stream of apologies and soul wrenching pleas for forgiveness into the black and golden center of the poppy in front of her. It thrummed and pulsed, it bent in the wind and brushed the backs of her hands. At one point, she lay on her back, allowing the tears to roll back across her temples as that same poppy bent to kiss her cheeks with each phantom gust of wind.

She wept as she reached into its magic for a countless time, and separated the smoky floral scent of magic from the rest. She pushed it to the side and let the earthy taste of moss and soil roll across her tongue, and she shattered.

She roared all her pain and anger into the empty blankness of the sky as she let Narcos's magic wash over her, flooding her senses and drowning her shame. Her voice cracked out, but the roaring remained. Panting and dizzy, she frantically looked around as the roar became deafening.

Thahaos reappeared beside her, throwing his body over hers as the gray of the sky ripped above her flame and ash raining down around them. Her view of the sky disappeared as Thahaos moved to cover her fully. The ground shook beneath them as she breathed in Thahaos's scent, the same smoke and floral smell as the poppy magic. After several moments, stillness filled The Blooming Gate again, and the God moved from his protective crouch.

She only had a breath to take in the entirely normal gray sky and field of poppies before she was crushed against a leather clad chest, the crisp scent of autumn filling her senses. Cal moved back, cradling her face in his palms, eyes scanning her frantically. His face broke into a blinding smile before he pulled her to him, crashing his lips to hers. One of his hands slid into the hair at her nape while the other fell to her hip, pulling her body flush with his and tilting her head to deepen his claiming kiss.

When he finally stopped for air, resting his forehead on hers, she chuckled softly.

"That doesn't count because I'm dead and this isn't my real mouth," she said, kissing his nose.

She panted a laugh and stepped back, allowing Lia to see the full scene for the first time. Othis was curled in the poppies several paces away, and just beside him was Wil, standing close to her father. His hand lay gently on her shoulder as they spoke too low for their words to travel.

Once Thahaos had uttered the words 'my daughter', she had known, how could she not. Wil was a mirror image of Miana. In the temple, she had the thought, but knew there were endless explanations, none of which were hers to know. She had never known of the Gods to have offspring, but somehow it seemed fitting for that to be the answer to Wil's mystery.

Wil looked up, swirling white eyes meeting depthless black, and motioned for Lia and Cal to join them. She felt Cal's hand on the small of her back as they moved through the poppies, like he was afraid she would vanish into the mist.

"Ahbba says that The Hunt took you somewhere to bathe and dress before you were taken to the hall where Cal found you?"

Lithia scrunched her nose. "Yes, this awful female took me to a small bed chamber, why?"

Wil nodded. "We need to find your body when we return. Do you think that's somewhere she could have taken it?"

"Well, there was a bed, so I don't see why not, though I can't imagine them caring much what happened to my body."

"We are sure they would have taken care to protect it. You dying was not a part of their plan as far as we know."

Thahaos stepped to her side, placing a heavy hand on her shoulder. "Lithia and I have been discussing the events between when she left my temple and when she arrived here. We believe that the only way to heal Suviel's magic is to forge it once more into a single heart."

Cal tensed at her side. "She is not touching that shard again."

She leaned into him slightly. "I will. This time, though, I am going to take all of the magic, not just the curse. We have to stop this, Calcas."

Lia could hear his teeth as they ground together in an effort to hold back whatever anger he had building.

Wil watched her for several minutes.

"Well, that certainly complicates this plan as a whole. We need to get in, find your body, and get back out. If we need to deal with the magic as well, that means we need a reason to linger."

Wil's eyes cut above Lia to Cal. "It's a good thing we have one then, isn't it?"

Cal's hand dropped from her back, and he moved away from her, slightly severing the contact he had kept since stepping into The Beneath.

"We are going to have to convince her not only that I have agreed to help, but that we retrieved Lia's soul for her, *and* convinced her to help. She's never going to believe you, Calcas."

"Who are you talking about, Wil?"

Cal spoke over her, "Is it possible to do it without revealing Lia?"

"No, they will sense her soul as soon as it's reunited. We could cloak it while she is without her body, but once she is reunited with her flesh, there is nothing I can do. Not to mention, we don't know what kind of watch they have on her body."

"Who?"

"Then we are going to have to convince her she is needed for the spell."

"All you would have to do is make her believe that Lia thinks we are healing the curse."

"YOU WILL NOT IGNORE ME!" Lia bellowed.

Cal's shoulders curled inward, and Thahaos stepped into Lia, curling his arm tightly around her shoulders.

"Daughter, please, one of you must tell her, then tell us all you know. I can not reach The Hunt, but we know they are involved."

"Cal, who are you talking about?" Lithia paused for a moment, thoughts clicking rapidly into place. "How...how are you here? Did you escape?"

"No, Lia. She let me go."

"Who, Calcas?"

He inhaled deeply, sadness flooding his eyes. "Seren."

LITHIA

The ground beneath her turned to quicksand, and her knees buckled. Before she began to fall, strong arms were there steadying her, bearing her weight. Her head spun around the name as she searched the faces in front of her. Wil's lip curled, her fist clenched and unclenched at her side. Over her shoulder, Thahaos's face was blank, a muscle ticking in his jaw.

She tried to turn to Cal, but the arms around her tightened, keeping her in place.

"How?"

It came out strangled plea, but it was the only word she could force through her teeth. Wil sucked air through her teeth like before opening her mouth, intending to speak, but Thahaos's hand landed heavy on her shoulder, stalling her.

"Seren is currently the leader of The Hunt, little queen."

The deep layers of his voice washed over her, and the apology threaded through his voice soothed the beginning roil of anger in her gut. She stared at the God, blinking, sifting through questions thundering through too fast for her to latch onto just one. Thahaos gestured towards the poppies at their feet.

"Sit."

They sat in tandem, Cal keeping his place close to her, his warm hand landing like a leaden weight on her thigh. Lia stared ahead at Thahaos, absently rubbing a velvet red petal between her fingers.

"I am sorry for not telling you sooner, Mo Bhanrighit," he started. "Not knowing the extent of The Hunt's involvement or what was happening on the surface, I thought it best not to speculate in a way that would distress you further."

Lia nodded absently for several minutes before finally looking to Cal again for the first time since he said her name.

"What is happening, Calcas?"

He ran his hand roughly through his hair, pulling his knee up to his chest and staring into the sea of red. Then, slowly, he spent the next hours detailing to both Lithia and Thahaos every part of Ser's plan.

As his story came to the point where he and Wil reunited in the valley, Lithia became aware of the world around her. The sky over The Blooming Gate was no longer empty and gray but roiling with black thunderheads. The poppies bent in a heavy wind, and the air was thick with the sense of a storm just on the precipice of breaking.

She looked to Thahaos in panic, tears streaked his deep brown skin, and as his facade flickered, she saw mirrored streams of red on his skeletal form. Lithia's hair whipped into her eyes, and as she moved it across her cheek, she found fresh tears on her own face.

Thunder cracked and Thahaos roared.

"SEREN! RETURN WHEN I SUMMON YOU."

The wind lashed violently, the smell of smoke and sulfur filling her senses. Wil moved towards her father, grasping his hands, forcing his attention from the sky to the steady calm of her white eyes. The wind stilled as quickly as it started. Calcas reached for her hand, but she flinched away. It was too much to add his touch to the feelings crashing around her.

Wil spoke quietly to Thahaos, the sky clearing slowly but remaining dark. After several minutes, she made her way to where Lia waited, an island in a sea of red.

"We need to go. Ahbba is going to continue to try to summon The Hunt. It seems as though this magic has given them some control over their tethers to The Beneath, so they are able to reject the summons."

Lia nodded. "He tried days ago, and they didn't answer then either."

Wil nodded. "They shouldn't be able to ignore a summons, delay if they are with a soul...but not ignore. Come on, we need to go before this gets worse."

Cal shifted, brushing her arm, and it took all of Lithia's willpower not to shift away from the touch. The touch was too much, it was all too much. Her eyes drifted to Othis, and panic gripped her heart as she realized how they would be leaving.

"Can Othis carry all three of us?"

Her voice rose as she spoke, anxiety clawing her throat. Wil smiled softly, her eyes searching Lia's.

"While he could, and he would be offended at your doubt, I feel I must remind you that you are not alive at present. You won't be riding Othis with us, I'll transport your soul. You will only remember being here, then being awake in your body again."

Lithia inhaled deeply the smoke and floral scent of The Blooming Gate, and nodded once. Wil's eyes pulsed with magic for a moment before there was blackness.

CALCAS

Cal watched as Lia faded from his line of sight for what felt like the hundredth time recently. A few moments after her soul disappeared, one of the rich black feathers on Willow's armor began to pulse and glow. He felt his jaw slacken as Wil's chuckle reached his ears. He looked up into her eyes, which still pulsed with magic.

"I have her, Cal, let's go," she said with a small smile.

He stared at the pulsing feather for several seconds before he finally started moving toward Othis.

Seated behind Wil, he braced himself for the sensation of tearing through the veil into The Beneath once more. Othis shot them skyward with a mighty beat of his wings. The poppies blurred into an endless streak of red, far ahead of them, a chasm slashed across the landscape, cutting it in two. Before they reached it, the amphiptere angled sharply upward, bellowing a rainbow of fire into the sky, burning a hole in the veil.

Like before, as they passed through, he could see the rip already healing at the edges. With a flash of blinding sunlight, they burst through the circular door of the temple and into the blinding morning sun pouring over the mountain peaks.

Othis made sweeping circles in the foggy morning sky before landing softly and letting them slip off his back. Wil pressed her forehead to his gleaming scales for several minutes before he took off, making the dust swirl around them.

Cal looked around, finding the entrance to the cave was only a few paces away, and he looked back at Wil, worry thick in his throat.

"This feels too—"

"I know. I told you before we left Cal, retrieving her soul would be the easy part; I do not expect it to get easier. I also do not expect her to be mad at you forever, she got a lot of information very quickly and had no time to process any of it."

Cal nodded curtly, not intending to talk about the hurt that had lodged itself in his heart when she flinched away from him and grew sharper with each beat. He turned and started toward the cave opening, Wil's near silent footsteps followed closely behind.

They made their way through the small sanctuary chamber, and he stopped to allow Wil to take in the mosaic that he now knew depicted her father. As she stared up, he found the small indentation in the center of the spiral, pressing his finger to it and allowing the stone to draw his blood.

The pit in his stomach sank and grew heavier with each step they took toward what he knew lay below. As they rounded the last curve in the hall and stepped into the garden, instead of the tranquil emptiness he had left several days ago, he found himself faced with several fully armored fae.

At the front of their formation, wearing the imposing crowned helm he knew was the marker of her station, was Seren. She was...calm. Both hands folded on the hilt of her sword, waiting for them. They stood staring into the darkness of her helm for several minutes as the tension thickened.

"I have to admit, Wil, I wasn't sure he could get you here." Her voice was slightly muffled by the helm's faceplate, but it was unmistakably her. Wil stared at Seren, and Cal saw the moment her mask slipped into place, though he doubted anyone else saw it for what it was. Her shoulders loosened slightly, eyes softening.

"Neither was I."

"I didn't expect you to come back at all, much to be honest. At least not without some plan to kill me...again."

"Seren, please..."

"Fine. Come."

She turned on her heel, to the clatter of armor as those gathered behind her moved to make room on the narrow path. Cal and

Wil exchanged a heavy look and followed, The Hunt closing ranks behind them.

To Cal's surprise, Ser led them to the small dining room where they had dined a few nights prior, indicating to the others not to follow before closing the door firmly behind her. She turned, and as she removed her helm, her armor dissolved to soft leathers.

They sat around the small table. Ser melted into her seat, her shoulders sagging slightly. Wil sat, hands folded in front of her, back straight, everything in her posture seemed calculated to look like deference, but Cal knew she was coiled as tightly as he was. Both of them were ready to move the moment the meeting turned sour.

Ser sighed, "You came." Her voice was warmer than he expected. "Both of you."

Neither of them replied. Cal shifted in his seat, leaning his weight onto the table, bowing his head to her stiffly.

"Why?"

Wil raised a dark brow. "Because your foolishness is unraveling the world, Seren. You *know* this isn't stable. And you know you're running out of time."

Ser's jaw clenched, and Wil leaned in, power rolling off her in waves.

Her voice lowered to a conspiratorial hush. "You messed up, though, because you need her alive or the magic will decimate everything. It needs the resistance of her magic."

Cal tamped down the confusion that threatened to overtake his features.

Ser snapped, spine snapping straight, "I didn't intend for her to die."

"But you need her," Cal said gently, eyes flitting to Wil, and the way the words landed made Ser flinch. "You said it yourself, this is about restoring everything. That has to rely on her magic."

Silence.

Then Ser stood, pacing slowly behind her chair, and ran her hand across the back of it, fingers tapping the smooth surface.

Wil let the quiet stretch just enough before glancing at Cal and standing. "I'm going to bring her back. We'll help you, but we need her to do it. She doesn't need to know everything, and I don't think she would agree to help if she did. She just needs to think she is here to finish what she started."

"I still..." Ser faltered slightly. "You already have her. Her soul, you already retrieved it, that's why Thahaos is summoning us."

They both froze. Cal looked to Wil, panic leeched its way through his skin, sinking into his bones. His muscles tensed, ready to move.

Wil smiled. "Of course we did, Seren. We were going to revive her whether you cooperated or not, but we would prefer to do this together."

"Why?"

"Why would I want to free my father from his eternal prison? Why would I want to see the world reunited through the death that had divided it for eons? If this spell works the way you claim, there won't be any thrones left to kneel before or balance left to keep. Just life, as it was before the veil, together in a place my father can walk with me."

Cal stared at Wil, finding himself pulled into her reasoning. He knew logically that this was her saying what Seren wants to hear, but he could hear a small, fractured kernel of truth in her words.

Ser's posture relaxed as she turned her honey gaze to Cal. "And you?"

Cal met her stare. "As I told you before, I've lost her too many times. I won't do it again. If this brings her back, I'll do what you need."

Ser considered a moment longer, then nodded once, decisively. "I'll take you to her body. We'll continue the spell once she has been returned to her body. But if she defies me—"

"She won't," Cal interrupted.

Ser hesitated, then stood, motioning to a small door at the back of the room.

"Come on then, she's not far."

As he turned to follow Ser, Wil caught his hand briefly in her own. It was cool and steady while his own was damp with sweat.

She squeezed it once, the feather at her throat pulsing, before they both turned and followed Seren through the low door.

LITHIA

The first breath was agony.

It licked like fire down her throat like a brand on her lungs, and blood seared as it tore through her veins. Her soul slammed into her flesh with such force that the world rocked as every particle of her being rushed to find its place. Her limbs spasmed. Cold. Then hot. Then everything all at once. Her heart stuttered in her chest before it settled into a rhythm. Her fingers curled, digging into thick velvet.

A bed.

She was on a bed. Not in The Beneath, a bed.

Shadows danced at the edge of her vision as she blinked the world into focus. Flickering light from the fireplace across the room stung her eyes. She blinked several times in an attempt to clear the dry, gritty feeling as she turned her head.

Wil was crouched at her side, hand still resting on Lia's chest. The feather on her shoulder glowed faintly, magic still tethered to her soul. Cal stood at the door, a silhouette of sharp lines.

"Don't try to speak yet. Welcome back."

Wil smiled at her, and she felt the delicate skin of her lips split as she smiled back.

"Ser isn't here. Calcas convinced her it was best that you woke without her in here. So far, it's going well, but I'm going to do what I can to heal you because things are about to move fast, and we need you."

She looked nervously at Cal before moving her hands to hover over Lia, the warm light of her magic glowing between them. Cal moved towards them, holding a waterskin to her lips. She drank greedily, the cool water dousing the raging heat that was shredding her from the inside with each breath.

Lia had no idea how long they had been in the small chamber, but she knew that Ser wouldn't leave them alone much longer. She was seated on the side of the bed, Wil braiding her now damp hair into a neat plait down her back.

After hours of magical healing and sleep, she had finally pulled herself from the bed and been able to bathe...slowly. Her body felt wrong. Like it didn't fit quite right anymore. The magic in her veins throbbed with more heat than she remembered, like it had been altered by her time in The Beneath.

The light in the garden was brighter than the small chamber they had been sequestered in for hours. Lithia's fresh eyes throbbed as she stepped through the door onto the stone pathway. She could feel her body still knitting itself back together. She just wanted to rest, but she knew they needed to do the next part quickly. The thought of looking into Seren's eyes again made her stomach twist into knots. And lying to her...Lithia pushed the guilt to the back corner of her mind.

She had to do what was best for all of them, including Seren, even if it meant tearing her plans to shreds. They followed the gently curling path towards the center of the garden, flanked on all sides by the looming guards she now understood to be The Hunt. The extremely disagreeable female who collected her from the cells was directly in front of her. She was tall, with broad shoulders that dipped in a near swagger as she walked. Lithia watched as she rolled a coin between her fingers, listening to the gentle clink against her gauntlets. The sound set her teeth on edge.

As they made the final turn to the center courtyard of the garden, the tall female flipped the coin up into the air and watched it spin. She caught it and smiled darkly at it before stepping to the side to allow them to pass. As Lithia moved past her, the smell of her magic landed like ash and rot on her tongue. Without much choice, she kept moving, turning her back to the vile guard, her eyes landing finally on the much more imminent threat in front of her.

Seren stood in black leathers, accented in the same opaline as the surrounding armor. Under her arm, she clutched a helm similar to the one emblazoned on every breastplate surrounding her. Glittering opaline and crowned with tall spikes, forming a terrifying silhouette. Lithia stared into her honey eyes and expected to find the same warmth and depth she always saw in them, but what she found instead was a wall. Lithia bit down on her tongue and attempted to shove down the frustration burning like bile in her throat.

"Welcome back, Lia."

The voice stopped her heart beating, the warm honey tone encasing it and trapping it like a fly in amber. Then Seren smiled. It wasn't a kind smile, it wasn't laced with emotion or longing. It was calculated, slashing. Lithia nodded once and painted a smile onto her face.

Cal approached Ser slowly, bowing his head. "We have done what we could to recover her strength in addition to returning her soul to her body."

Ser's gaze flicked over Cal, then to the simmering nebula of magic in the center of the courtyard. The void was slipping around the stars like oil. Lithia kept her features gently blank, so when Seren's eyes settled back on her, she found a carefully crafted illusion.

"Are you all ready then? Best move quickly before the magic breaks down further."

Lia knew she was the response Ser was looking for. Knew she was watching for any slip, any wrong word, and a fracture in their brittle lie.

"I am still recovering," she offered. Her voice was quiet but strong. "My time in The Beneath did not come without cost, but Wil has assured me that the spell only needs my magic. I have the strength enough for that. I will do what is needed to save my queendom."

Ser's jaw ticked, and Lithia felt the small ripple as every fae in the courtyard tensed slightly at the strength in her declaration. She held her body perfectly still, worried any movement would shatter the fragile peace.

Ser motioned towards the shard, and Lithia heard Wil let out a small breath beside her. She turned, and Wil held out a hand to her. She knew it was part of the ruse of Wil needing to borrow

Aduna's magic, but the steady warmth of Wil's hand calmed her racing heart as they moved toward the pulsing magic. All they had to do now was hope they didn't kill Lia a second time when they realized what was happening.

They came to a stop on the same spot Lia had stood days earlier when she attempted to rip the curse from the shard. Wil made a small show of allowing her magic to build, vibrating the air around them. She spoke quickly and quietly for only Lia to hear.

"I'm going to drop your hand in a moment, you need to be quick. Cal and I will protect you once they realize something is wrong." She raised her voice so the others could hear. "Cal, can you come let her lean on you, she is weak."

In a heartbeat, there was a strong body at her back.

"What are you doing, Wil?" came Seren's voice, a note of panic lacing her tone.

Cal kissed the top of Lia's head and turned, his back to hers, and she heard the gentle scrape of metal on leather as he slid his morningstar from its sheath.

Wil dropped her hand, turning on the spot.

Lithia moved.

She plunged her hands into the swirling stars, twisting her fingers in the white hot strands of magic and anchoring them to her. She took a deep breath, the taste of night blooming jasmine flooding her senses, and she pulled.

There was a blinding flash of white light, and Lithia felt her magic shred and heal itself over and over as she syphoned the magic, bringing it into herself. The light faded, and she blinked hard several times, trying to keep her balance. There was total silence behind her.

She turned to find total chaos frozen in time. Everyone stared at her in stages of shock.

Ser's jaw clicked as she slammed it closed, sucking panting breaths through her teeth."

She prowled closer to Lia.

"You—" she hissed. "You lied."

Lia moved forward, her strength returned tenfold, power roaring through her veins. "And you killed me, Seren."

The dam broke and chaos erupted again.

Calcas

Cal whipped the morningstar in a circle as the armored wraith in front of him lunged forward. He caught their breastplate with a sickening crunch, the spikes denting the gleaming armor and puncturing its shell. To his right, Wil threw up a wall of swirling black feathers, her magic sweeping several of The Hunt off into the crystalline water. His shadow writhed and curled up his body, punching out at another fae charging toward him.

He reached for his waist with his free hand, gripping the warm hilt of Lithia's sword. The dragon glass sang as it slid free of its scabbard. He ducked a blow aimed for his head, sliding the sword toward Lia as he spun out of the way. She knelt, power pulsing from her hand as soon as her fingers wrapped around the hilt.

She stood again, facing Seren, the two of them an island of calm wrath in the midst of a storm. The air around Lia began to hum, the tension growing before something yielded. The ground cracked beneath them and began to shake. A scream tore from Lithia's throat as magic that glittered like the night sky burst from her, forming enormous wings on her back and causing the air around them to churn as the cavern buckled around them.

"We could have been Gods," Seren spat, fury morphing her beautiful features into something monstrous.

"I would rather die a mortal than live in your nightmare."

Magic exploded from Lithia in a shower of stars, and Seren roared. The other members of The Hunt began to fade out one by one. The large female who led them to the garden flipped her coin and scowled at it before locking eyes with Cal and sneering and leaving like the others. The wind created by Lia's magic whipped Seren's hair into her face as she yelled over the building storm, her eyes fixed on Calcas.

"You know this is the only option, Cal."

A mighty roar sounded overhead, and the simmering black amphiptere swooped in from somewhere above them. It didn't stop as it approached Seren, and she grabbed hold of its saddle mounting as it circled the courtyard. She stared at Lia, and something in her eyes softened, the cracks in her walls showing, before she looked back to Cal and smirked.

The amphiptere took off upward, roaring a column of white hot flame into the sky, tearing a hole in the realm that Seren disappeared into.

Calcas shared a worried look with Wil as they watched Lia. The magic around her was palpable, radiating from her body in waves. The air around them began to calm, plunging them into a peaceful quiet. The three of them stared at each other for several minutes as the magic around Lia cooled.

"You have wings."

Lia chuckled at his quiet observation. "Apparently."

"Tadhg is going to be so annoying." He said with a scowl.

This pulled a real laugh from her and a chuckle from Wil. He stared at the wings, they were similar to the ones she had conjured the night she syphoned his shadows, deep, iridescent black but pulsing and writhing at the edges, like they wanted to remind you they were made of magic, not flesh and cartilage. Lia gasped slightly, and the wings faded.

Wil was the first of them to move.

"Lia, do you need rest? We should leave for the others as soon as possible. I don't want to push you past your limits, but we shouldn't linger here either."

Lia looked at her body as if checking she had all her limbs.

"I'm okay, we should go."

Cal stepped to her, reaching out a hand to move the hair from her face. She stepped away from his touch, and the pain in his heart burrowed deeper. He smiled at her and bowed.

"I'm glad you are back, Mo Bhanrighit."

The formal words burned his tongue as he spoke. He removed her scabbard from his belt and handed it to her, turning and starting down the path. Logically, he knew she just needed the space, but all he wanted to do was touch her. He needed to feel she was safe. See her flesh dimple beneath his fingers and know that she is real and alive and...he shook the spiral from his thoughts and swallowed the thick feeling in his throat.

He heard the soft scuff of boots behind him and didn't look back.

Cal stared out at the moonlight reflecting off the smooth, still surface of Lake Clotho. They had only been back for a day, but Lia had avoided all unnecessary contact with him. Granted, she had slept for half of that time, the fatigue of that much magic passing through her newly healed body finally catching up to her once she felt safe.

"I don't hate you, Cal."

He breathed in deeply, listening to her soft footfalls and the swish of fabric as she sat in the chair behind him. He didn't turn from the window, afraid that if he did, he would realize she was in his imagination. He let the silence settle, nearly convincing himself she truly wasn't there, when she spoke again.

"I'm sorry. My first response was to pull away from you when it should have been to hold on."

He turned around, leaning against the cool stone sill and crossing his legs at the ankle. She looked better, the flush was back in her pale cheeks, her fiery copper hair was neatly braided away from her face. He traced the long line of her neck with his eyes, following her runes where they vanished into the black stain of the void that had ripped her from the world.

"It's not your fault, Lia, don't add me to the pile of things weighing you down. I understand."

"I know you do." She said with a small smile, "You are my mate after all."

Cal let out a heavy breath. "I panicked, Lia, I felt you die, and she immediately took you from me, and I just—I would have done anything in that moment to get you back. I can't keep losing you, but I don't want you to feel like fate has taken yet another choice away from you, the way your station has."

Lia watched him, her nose scrunched. "You think I wouldn't choose you."

"I think you have gotten to choose precious little in your life, and I want you to be able to choose who you love. This bond feels like wading into The Idris with a pocket full of stones, Lia, and I refuse to drown you."

"I have chosen who I love, Calcas. I chose to love Ser, it wasn't fate's choice, it was mine. I chose to marry Narcos, the love was different, but I—" She sucked in a reagent breath, wiping furiously at her eyes like they betrayed her. "I found his soul in The Blooming Gate. Thahaos was teaching me to separate magic, to control my syphon, and I found his magic, I knew its taste and texture. I finally said all the things I needed to say to his soul and...I did love him, Cal, not the way he deserved to be loved, but I loved him and I chose him." She sniffled and laughed.

"I may not have chosen him to be my consort, mother did that, but I did choose to find peace with him. You are right that I haven't gotten to choose so many parts of my story, but no matter what, Cal, I will always choose you. I have chosen your friendship for my entire life, and I won't stop choosing you now."

He watched her in silent shock for a moment, her words crashing through his mind. "Friendship, I can do th—"

Her quiet laugh bounced through the air, cutting him off.

"Calcas, you have to stop doing that, you aren't drowning me, you are drowning yourself in my name, and you can't keep doing that. I do not want to be your friend, I *want* to be your mate. I *want* my mate to be my oldest friend. I *want* my mate to be the same fae I ran through the Citadel with as a youngling. I *want* my mate to be *you*, Calcas, don't minimize it out of fear. I am not afraid."

LITHIA

The silence vibrated with years of tension that never had room to dissipate. Buried grief and lost time and the terrible ache of what-ifs clogged the air between them. Then it shattered, and Cal was moving. Before she could take a full breath, he was kneeling in front of her, and his mouth was on hers.

It wasn't patient or gentle. It was a raw and desperate all-consuming thing. It tasted like years of moments stolen by war and too big choices that were made too fast. His hands cradled her face, slipping into her hair and drawing her closer as though he was afraid she would vanish again.

So she chased his fear, kissing him back fiercely, arching off the chair into his chest, she fisted her hands in the soft linen of his shirt. With one hand, he gripped the hair at her nape harder while his other fell to her thigh and began slowly hiking the simple material of her nightdress up her leg.

She pulled him into her, gripping his torso with her legs, tasting panic and hunger on his lips, feeling the deep tremble beneath his skin. He broke the kiss and pressed his forehead against hers, his breath ragged, fingertips dimpling the bare flesh of her thigh.

"I wanted to trust her, Lia," Cal whispered.

Lithia blinked several times, her heart pounding like war drums. "W-What?"

"I had just felt you die, and I wanted to believe she could fix it," he said, his thumb stroking along her jaw. "What she was offering was a way to undo it all, undo the death and the pain, to bring you back...I wanted to believe her. Not because I thought it was right, or good, or even sane."

Lithia sat frozen, knuckles white against the soft black of his shirt.

"But you knew what she was asking was impossible. You had to—"

"I *knew*," he interrupted, dejected, "but Lia, there wasn't any logic left in me. I'd lost you, and when I felt the thread between us begin to fray, when I *knew* you were gone, I unraveled too."

His hands moved in tandem, sliding across her shoulders and down her arms before gripping her hips and bunching in the soft green fabric of her nightdress.

"I kept telling myself that I was strong enough to stand against her if the time came. That, I was only going along with any of it to buy time to get to Wil and the others for help. But that isn't the truth. The tru—the truth is, I would have chosen you over the world in that moment, Lithia, and she was the voice saying I could have you."

Lithia swallowed, emotion catching in her throat. "Cal—"

"I hate myself for it, Lia."

He laughed bitterly. "Even as I stood there, pretending to be disgusted and angry, the voice in my head kept whispering *what if*. What if tearing the veil down really could fix it all? What if we could start the world over again? What if we didn't have to bear the weight of loss?"

Her heart ached for the quiet torment he'd carried while she floated between death and magic.

She felt where his heart beat wild and fast beneath her hand. She traced the strong line of his jaw and ran the pad of her thumb down the ring that split his bottom lip.

"We all crave a softer ending when the truth is sharp," she said softly. "You are worthy of my choice, Calcas. I could never punish you for needing hope, even if you found it in the wrong place."

He bent his head, nuzzling it into her lap as his shoulders shook. She ran her fingers along his scalp, where his hair, usually short on the sides, had started to grow out slightly. After several minutes, he turned his head to the side, capturing her arm and laying soft kisses on the inside of her wrist.

He looked up into her eyes, with damp tracks on his cheeks, and smiled.

"Did you know you have stars in your eyes now? Like the shard can't help but look out."

Lia smiled as he kissed her again, slower this time, less frantic. Lithia could feel the weight on their bond lift, not vanish entirely, but lighten. Cal slipped his hands under her thighs and stood, lifting her off the chair. Lia wrapped her legs around his waist, the thin material of her nightdress bunching at her hips.

He carried her across the floor in quick strides and deposited her on the soft mattress that dipped and shifted as he crawled over her, placing small kisses on her exposed flesh and nipping at her collarbone. The skin of his hands was rough and calloused as he pulled frantically at the thin straps, freeing her arms and exposing her breasts to the cool air of the room.

"Cal—" The beginning of her plea came out breathless, and a wolfish grin curled the corner of Calcas's mouth. "Please, you can be slow about it next time."

"Anything for you, Mo Bhanrighit."

He grinned as he pulled his shirt over his head, and she lifted her hips so he could pull her nightdress the rest of the way off her body. He stood and hooked his hands around the backs of her knees and dragged her to the edge of the bed, lowering himself to drape her leg over his shoulder. He left a hot line of kisses on the inside of her thigh, causing her breath to hitch.

She felt his smile on her skin for a fraction of a second before his tongue was there with a long, slow stroke to her heated flesh, drawing a needy moan from her throat. She arched into his mouth and felt him chuckle as his tongue moved to strong, steady circles around her clit, and she ground further into his face.

He reached one hand up and pressed down lightly on her hips, holding her in place as he devoured her arousal. Panting as she felt her pleasure rise, just before it broke and washed over her, he stopped, leaving her nerves on fire, and liquid heat pooled at the base of her spine.

He stood quickly, freeing his hard cock from his pants and stroking it from base to tip several times. Through hooded eyes, she saw pre-cum beading just above the piercing and licked her suddenly dry lips. Her eyes traced up his muscular body, following the flowing shadows tattooed across his torso until they settled on his beautifully mismatched eyes.

He leaned in and kissed her deeply, swallowing her moan at the taste of her own arousal. She reached out and dug her nails into his hips, pulling his body to her, his hard length slipping through her wetness. Growling, he shifted, aligning himself before sinking into her in one long thrust. His head dropped to her shoulder as he stilled, breathing deeply.

Lithia groaned at the fullness, her walls fluttering at the intrusion. Lifting her legs, she locked them around his waist, shifting her hips to meet his thrusts as he began to move. There was nothing slow or tender. Cal drove into her in powerful thrusts, her nails digging into his back as she gasped and writhed beneath him.

Cal moved one of her legs to his shoulder, deepening the angle as his thumb moved to her clit and began circling in time with his thrusts. The overwhelming urge to let go overtook Lia's body as fire overtook her veins and the dam broke inside her. She cried out, and Cal's movements became more frantic before he stilled, growling and burying his face in her neck.

He panted, peppering her neck and shoulder with kisses. He slipped from her and helped her stand, sliding an arm around her waist. Her legs felt unsteady as he gripped the back of her neck and pulled her into another searing kiss. She leaned back in his arms and smiled before kissing the tip of his nose.

"Those kisses counted."

He laughed as she made her way to the washroom. He was still smiling as she slipped her nightdress back on and crawled under the blankets. He was still smiling as she curled into him, listening to his steady, even heartbeats. And she could still hear the small smile in his voice when he finally spoke again just before she fell asleep.

"I want to choose you, too, Lia."

Calcas

The bed beside him had been cool when he woke up the next morning. His initial reaction had been fear that she was still gone when he heard her voice outside his window, and the tension left his body in a breath.

When he finally made his way out into the blinding morning sun, he found Lithia sitting in the grass, legs crossed, facing Tadgh, and with her wings on full display. They were smiling and talking as Tadhg pointed to different points on her wings. The celestial fae had his shirt off, his scarred back on display. He stopped and watched them talk for several minutes, deciding to leave them and find Wil, when Lia saw him and smiled. So he made his way across the patchy grass to where they sat near the water.

"Tadhg was helping me figure out how the celestial magic feels and how to move it in my body."

Tadhg's grin was wide and bright.

"I was also trying to explain to her that she's a dragon and not an amphiptere," he said with a laugh.

Cal bit back a laugh at the memory of calling her a baby dragon to Tadhg when they spoke in Mt. Haven.

"Of course you're a dragon, you have arms and legs."

Lia rolled her eyes. "Like I told this one," she said, poking Tadhg and scrunching her nose, "I'm not a giant flying anything, I'm just another fae with wings, maybe if I start breathing fire later we can talk."

"Whatever you say, little dragon," Cal said, finally unable to swallow his laughter.

Amid their laughter and Lia's huffs of indignation, the calm surface of the lake began to roil. Tadhg and Lithia stood quickly, shifting to face the water as Aegaea's head broke the surface. Water glittered on her skin, scales gently shifting to skin as she rose from the churning lake.

Tadhg bent and snatched his shirt from the grass, jogging to meet her in the sand and offering her the thin linen when she finally dragged her feet free of the shallows. She took it with a smile, shaking the water quickly from her hair and body before slipping it over her head. She took several quick steps towards Lia and wrapped her arms tightly around her, speaking quietly in her ear. It took several moments, but Lia finally relented and returned the unexpected touch.

She stepped back onto the sand, pulling a large bag of books from the water, and nodded toward the house. She smiled sadly at Lia before speaking.

"I found something, but it'll be easier to tell you all at once."

"Neda and Wil are in the library already, possibly arguing, who knows, but I can take the books if you want to get dressed," Tadhg offered.

Aegea looked down at the shirt that was just grazing the top of her thighs and grinned back at Tadhg with faux innocence as she handed him the heavy bag.

"Do my legs make you nervous, healer?"

"Always. EGH! You could have dried the bag first!"

Her laugh was light and airy as she looped her arm through Lia's and started towards the house. "Those books have never been dry, why start now?"

Cal chuckled at the slightly green look Tadhg gave to the bag before slinging the strap over his chest.

"Calcas? Laughing? That's not the asshole I know."

Cal sent his shadows out to trip Tadhg as they crossed the threshold into the house. Tadhg made a slight choking sound as the bag caught his throat mid stumble.

"Don't further tempt me to drown you in The Idris."

As they approached the library, he could hear the soft noise from inside, indicating that Neda and Wil were indeed arguing about something. He pushed on the slightly warped wood of the door, and it groaned as it scraped along the worn floorboards. Wil was sitting, massaging her temples while Neda stood, leaning across the table, her white-blonde hair blocking her face from view.

They both looked up at the sound of the door. The frustration in Neda's eyes deflated slightly at the sight of them, likely sensing she was about to lose whatever argument was being waged. Wil's tired expression, however, stayed as she spoke quietly.

"It doesn't matter what I think in the end, wildheart, we need to talk to everyone and make a plan. This is just a piece of a much larger plan."

Neda's fists clenched, knuckles blanching on the tabletop before she sat hard in her chair.

"Aegaea is back," Tadhg said, plopping the wet bag into the nearest chair with a squelch.

Wil and Neda both sat up straighter, shaking off their argument in favor of the simple escape Tadhg offered, and spoke rapidly over each other.

"What did she say?"

"Did she find anything?"

Cal shook his head, squeezing Wil's shoulder on his way to the chair on her left. "Don't know. She said she would tell us all together. I would say yes, though, because knowing her, she wouldn't have come back empty handed."

Wil nodded, eyes glazing.

Tadhg sank into the chair across from Cal and leaned into Neda. "And what were you love birds arguing about?"

The front legs of the chair Tadhg was sitting in suddenly sank into the stone, sending him spilling onto the floor under the table. Wil chuckled softly beside Cal as they watched him crawl back into the chair and act like nothing happened.

He rubbed the spot on his chest that made contact with the table as he spoke again, coughing slightly. "What were you guys talking about? Did you figure something out?"

Neda offered him a venomous smile as she answered, "Possibly." She turned that same smile on Wil. "But it needs to be factored into the plan at large."

Wil sighed at his side, and he could feel the weight of her exhaustion. The library doors groaned open again to reveal Lia and Aegaea, their hair braided similarly in mismatched shades of copper and deep red. Aegaea had put on a pair of tan leggings but was still wearing Tadhgs's shirt and no shoes. She stopped at the end of the table nearest the door and shifted the books from the chair to the floor before sitting, while Lia rounded to the far end of the table, dropping a new shirt in Tadhg's lap as she passed.

They sat in heavy silence for several minutes until Lithia finally spoke.

"Okay. What's next?"

No dwelling, no lamenting or anger, or wallowing in perceived failure, just forward movement. He wasn't sure that was something he would have been able to do in her place. In fact, history was a pretty decent indicator that he would, in fact, run the other direction if given the opening.

"I think I know where the Tidal Court's shard is. When Cal described the sanctuary in the cave you came across, I realized I knew of a place like it."

Cal realized he was enormously grateful for Aegaea's proclivity to get directly to a point.

"There is a place in the sea, it's between Twin Harbors and the tip of Nightstone Island. It was a temple to the Salt Goddess. She's a minor deity, and we don't keep the temple anymore as we all worship Aduna, but there is a mosaic chamber like the one you described."

Lithia leaned forward eagerly. "That's perfect, Aegaea."

Aegaea grimaced. "It is, but there are a couple of major problems. First, it's deep. Deeper than most of us tend to go, and you, my dears, are lacking the fins. Second, because it's been abandoned so long, it's been inhabited by a herd of necsite. While that usually would be the smallest problem, it's a fairly large problem with the voiding. We have no idea the state they are in."

Cal saw Lia tense and slid his hand across the table to lace his fingers with hers. She gripped his hand with bruising strength, her jaw locked in place and her eyes focused on Aegaea.

"What else?" Wil asked, her voice a whisper of apprehension.

Aegaea winced slightly. "It's at the bottom of the whirlpool."

The air in the room stilled.

"I assume you knew all of these things, and that's why you left?" Lia asked quietly.

Aegaea nodded. "I came back with a plan."

LITHIA

"Run me through it again."

Aegaea nodded to Lia, rubbing slightly at her tired eyes. All the papers on the table had been moved to make space for the damp tomes Aegaea was referencing as she explained her plan to them.

"I have a ship on the way; it should arrive tomorrow. It will take about three days by ship to get from here, down the Idris, through Soundless Bay and the Twin Harbors, and to Nightstone."

She locked eyes with Lithia, waiting for acknowledgment before she continued. Lia nodded once.

"The whirlpool shifts with the tides, so high tide will be the best option we have. If we enter the water from Nightstone and descend there, we should be able to get to the bottom and then approach the temple at the narrowest part of the whirlpool. The only part we can't really plan for is the necsite. If they aren't void touched, they shouldn't be much of a problem, but if they are—"

"I know," Lia bit out.

Lithia was surprised to find that no one's face contained pity, only understanding, and it soothed the guilt that burned the back of her throat. She silently thanked Thahaos that the fear she felt was lighter than she expected as well.

"I'll be able to give you the air to get down there." She glanced around the table, eyes settling on Cal. "I can only do it for one, so if everyone comes, it will double our size because we will need a tidal fae for each of you, and I won't force any of them into that choice."

"Of course not," Lia agreed. "How are we getting through the whirlpool, though, even at a narrow point?"

Aegaea tilted her head back and forth. "The way the current works, it drags down. I think if we enter the current above the temple and swim for the eye as we descend, we should be able to make it to the entrance."

"And if you miss?" Neda asked, a wrinkle between her brows.

"We can't miss," she replied simply.

Neda's expression morphed into a scowl, and Aegaea smiled softly.

"If the temple has always been there, then it is doable. I have a feeling it was designed by the Salt Goddess to be this way. Enter from the top of the whirlpool the way a non-tidal fae would, and the whirlpool will consume you. Tidal fae are taught as younglings to escape the dangers of the deep, it is part of us."

A strange look crossed Aegaea's face.

"Now that I think about it, though, I suspect the whirlpool exists because of the shard. They likely built the temple there, not knowing what they were building on top of. I wonder if it will remain once you take the shard."

Wil leaned back in her chair, leaning on her elbow and running her thumb along her bottom lip as she spoke.

"It may. The Celestial Shard was surrounded by a garden of plants I've never seen outside their floating cities, that shouldn't survive on Suviel's surface, floating trees, night lilies, star grass. It was all still intact when we left. It's possible the echo of the magic is strong enough to sustain it. It's also possible it will wither with time."

"If it fades, I'll see if father can start a new one. I don't want the temple to lose its protection. I suspect it wouldn't do to let the prisoners on Nightstone think it was safe to try to swim away either, since it blocks the narrowest point between Nightstone and the mainland."

"Gooooooooood point," said Tadhg from where he was lying across his chair with his legs crossed at the ankle, head on one armrest, eating a large chunk of bread.

Neda scoffed at him. "Well, since it would take a lot of effort to get us all to the bottom, can I suggest something to cover more ground at once?"

Lia sat back in her chair and motioned for Neda to continue, eager for anything that would speed up this process.

"I am fairly sure the Hearth Shard is in Fermholme at the Tree of Beginnings. I need to speak to Nylian so we can work out where exactly and how to get to it. He would know more, being the Prime and having been heir his whole life."

Lia nodded. "You want to go to Fernholme while we get the Tidal Shard."

Neda nodded. "If you, Cal, and Aagaea go to the Tidal Shard, the rest of us can go to Fernholme. You can meet us there, the ports in Hearth are the closest to Nightstone."

"It will take you about the same amount of time to reach Fernholme as it will take us to get to Nightstone. You won't have too much of a lead on us."

Neda looked to Wil, who shook her head and sighed.

"Not if we leave now."

"Now?" Tadhg's exclamation was punctuated by his boots smacking the floor.

Neda ground her teeth. "Yes, now, we sent a crow to the fort for your horses when you returned from The Beneath. They brought them this morning, we'll take them with us so we have them for whatever comes after Fernholme."

Cal nodded absently and reached over to squeeze her hand like he had earlier when Aegaea first mentioned the necsite.

"It's a good idea, if we concentrate our resources too much, we will waste time."

His low rumble soothed her quickly fraying nerves.

"The ship should be here in the morning anyway. There is no sense in wasting the riding time."

She searched his mismatched eyes for comfort before agreeing.

"It's a good plan, Neda, you'll need to leave soon to be clear of the valley before nightfall. How many horses do we have?"

Neda snapped into quick planning mode, like the general she was.

"Four. Tadhg wasn't in a state to ride alone when we returned, but he is fine now. So Tadhg can ride the legion horse Wil came on. If we pack our things on Daylis and Wil rides Redmaw, because Goddess knows he's not letting anyone else near him," she added under her breath, "we should be able to make great time."

Lia gave her a curt nod. "Go."

They all stood from the table, quiet goodbyes and good lucks, passing freely. Wil stopped and pressed her forehead silently to

Lia's. She didn't say anything at all, but it was everything Lia needed to hear.

The sun-bleached deck rocked lightly under her feet as she stared out at the shoreline of Lake Clotho just before sunrise. Cal was laughing loudly with a group of sailors he seemed to know, while Aegaea spoke quickly and quietly with the male Lia assumed to be the captain.

The ship was smaller than the larger ships she knew the Tidal fleet to contain. It was salt worn, with large, faded sails being unrolled to catch the morning breeze. The captain wasn't one she recognized. He was deeply sun tanned with brown hair knotted at his nape, a brimmed hat in his hand. He had the same seafoam green eyes as Aegaea and smiled broadly as she spoke.

She said something that made him laugh heartily, then he turned his blinding smile on Lia. They both started walking to where Lia waited at the bow.

The captain bowed low when he reached her. "Mo Bhan-righit."

Lia bowed shallowly back. "Captain."

"Please, call me Rayne," he offered as he flashed her the same warm smile. "While I am the captain, this crew isn't very formal, and the men will start to make fun of me."

"Rayne is my half-brother," Aegaea said with a soft smile. "Though he prefers to stay dry for whatever reason, just like father. His crew is good, if a bit...rough. They will get us there quickly, Lia."

The expression on Lia's face must have shifted because Aegaea laid a cool hand on her arm and squeezed before walking toward where Cal was laughing with the crew. Rayne watched her, turning to lean on the railing beside Lia.

"You know he sailed with us for a bit, a few years after the battle?"

Lia leaned beside him, wrapping her arms around herself, the uncomfortable feeling of being on the outside looking through fogged glass prickling her skin.

"No. I don't know much of anything that he did between that day and the marking a few weeks ago."

Rayne nodded, still smiling. "He looks a hell of a lot more like himself right now than he did then, which is interesting given the world is falling apart." He paused and his smile finally dropped into something more pained. "I won't tell you he was a good man then or that any of us are good men now, for that matter, but I think sometimes we rip ourselves apart to avoid the things that were made to hold us together. I'm glad he seems together again, even if the cracks are still visible."

Lia stared out at the water, not sure how to respond. It felt like Cal had allowed everyone to see him falling apart but her. Rayne looked over the railing towards the mouth of the river and nudged Lia.

She turned and saw the sun begin to break the horizon. Like a bolt of lightning splitting the sky it lit the reflective surface of the river, a glowing vein from the lake to the horizon. The light slowly dripped into the rest of the landscape, warming the cool blues of the early morning into liquid gold, filling the bowl of the valley.

"Time to go, Mo Bhanrighit."

"Lia," she said, not turning from the sunrise.

CALCAS

Cal watched the crew scurry up and down the ratlines as they navigated the rapid waters of the Idris with a practiced ease. The trip from the bay to Lake Clotho would have taken magic, going against such a strong current. With the current and full sails, however, the speed was nearly nauseating.

Cal, Lia, and Aegaea had spent the majority of the time since they left the morning before in Rayne's cabin, taking up all the space at his table, trying to figure out where exactly the Arcane Shard could be on Drake Mountain and how to get to it.

It was testing his patience, the mountain itself was vast and crawling with danger, and that had nothing on if the shard was near the crater of the volcano itself. He turned, leaning on the railing, and let the spray hit his face as the mouth of the bay approached. He needed to get through this shard with Lia intact before he could focus on the next.

He watched as the riverbank rose steadily, forming the high walls that carved out the bay. The sound of the river grew louder the closer they got to the bay, echoing off the cliff walls, vibrating through his bones. Few ships were allowed to traverse this portion of the Idris, the current here strong and dangerous on a good day, deadly on a bad one.

The river roared toward the opening that marked the entrance to Soundless Bay, all other sounds entirely drowned out by the clamor. He felt Lia slip up beside him, stepping silently into him as they watched the ship navigate the narrow passage, bursting into Soundless Bay. He wrapped an arm around her waist, pulling her into him as the roaring noise was replaced by a deafening silence that made his ears ring.

The quiet calm of the bay was always startling. His ears ached, and it took several minutes for the ringing to subside. The island of Arachin rose from the center of the bay, a plinth of stone holding the capital city towards the clouds. It loomed as they rounded the bay, passing under the bridge.

"It'll be a few hours before we reach the harbors. Sleep while you can," he said into Lia's hair, kissing her softly.

She straightened, looking at him wearily. "You are allowed to rest, too."

Cal rolled his eyes and unfurled his shadows, sending them creeping up her back to tangle in her braid, using them to pull her face to his, capturing her mouth in a claiming kiss.

As they pulled apart, the ship listed hard to one side, knocking them into the railing, the water heaving towards them. Cal's boots slid on the wet deck as he held onto the railing and Lia's waist. There was a chorus of clawing, scratching, and he scanned the deck looking for any indicator of what was coming, but the crew looked just as confused as he felt.

As the ship righted itself, he looked over the side and found dark shapes slithering up the side of the boat. He backed quickly toward the center of the deck, pulling Lia with him.

"Kapora?" It was Aegaea's sing-song voice that ordered his confusion. "Why are they boarding us? Why are they leaving the water at all?"

Slimy hands and tentacles covered in iridescent scales were followed over the railing by the small horned heads and lean bodies of a small band of kapora. Their usually soft, glowing eyes were pitch black, jaws overfull of sharp teeth barred in rage as they hissed at the crew.

"The void magic," Lis whispered at his side. "They shouldn't be a danger at all."

He heard swords slide from sheaths all around him as he reached back, freeing his morningstar from its place on his back. Near where Rayne was steering, two kapora were already lunging at the fae protecting him, a wail of agony shattering the fragile tension as one sank its sharp teeth into flesh.

Cal thrust his hand forward, fingers splayed, a fountain of flame erupting toward the first small creature that lunged at him. It shrieked and stumbled back, scaled skin bubbling and blistering. He didn't wait for it to fall, bringing his morningstar down in a crushing blow.

"Calcas, if you light my ship on fire, I'll kill you myself!" came Rayne's voice over the clamor of shrieks and fighting.

Cal shot him a rude gesture as another kapora dove at him, mouth wide open. He ducked, narrowly avoiding its teeth as it crashed into the barrels behind him with a dull thud. Across the deck, Lia moved like a storm, sword spinning. She moved low and quick, slicing through soft scales and dodging the sting of clawed hands. One lurched toward her, catching her arm as she cut through its throat, and she growled as the inky black blood oozed onto her skin.

She froze, and a loud crack split the air as magic burst from her chest, killing the few kapora around her in a heartbeat. The fight all around them stopped. A sound like a dying bird broke the silence, and the remaining kapora surged off the side of the deck and into the water.

Lithia crumpled.

"What was the noise before they fled?"

He spoke quietly, trying not to wake Lia. The ship was back to its usual creaking sway as they passed through the Twin Harbors. Lithia had collapsed quickly after the kapora attack and hadn't woken, and he wasn't sure what had caused it, but he was finally able to talk to Rayne and Aegaea now that the carnage had been cleaned up.

Rayne sighed. "It was a caller. Still a kapora, but it's normally a great ugly thing that stays in the water and watches for danger. It seems this one was doing the same, even though they were the aggressors. Whatever Lia did scared it enough to call them, so they left."

Aegaea was curled on the end of Lia's bed, with large bandages on her arm. She yawned before she started talking.

"I've never seen a kapora attack anything larger than a fish. Killing any of them hurts my heart." She sniffled slightly, and Rayne reached over to hold her hand. "Do you know what happened to Lia?"

Cal leaned his head back on the headboard. "Not really. I assume it was the magic use. It looked like celestial magic, and she hasn't had it long, so it's likely it was just too much."

Rayne stood from his chair at the foot of the bed. "We should be at Nightstone tomorrow, barring any further unexpected boardings. You all three should rest."

He leaned down and scooped Aegaea up into his arms and carried her out of the low door to her own cabin. Cal slid down into the bed, wrapping his body around Lia and listening to her steady breaths as the sea rocked him to sleep.

LITHIA

L ia woke with the warmth of Cal's chest beneath her cheek. She lay perfectly still, not wanting to wake him or ruin the peace before she absolutely had to.

"I know you're awake, little dragon."

She shifted to look up into his face. He smiled down at her, his eyes crinkling at the corners. He kissed her forehead softly, and she drew closer into his warmth.

"Do you know what happened?"

His voice vibrated her body as he spoke.

"No—" Her voice stuck in her dry throat. "I mean, I remember I tried to call on the celestial magic, but I think in the moment I just pulled on too much of it and it overwhelmed me. I just need to remember to balance the magic as I'm using it."

"That seems easier said."

She chuckled softly. "Possibly. I worked with Thahaos in The Beneath to focus when I syphon, it should be similar. I just need to be able to feel for the magic I need rather than allowing all my magic out at once."

"You practiced?"

Lia smiled. "I told him how I felt after Nars, the loss of control in a moment of need. I told him I never wanted to feel that again, and he understood. I think—I think he may have understood more than I realized. He had me practice on the poppies."

Cal was silent, and Lia looked up to find him looking at her with mild horror. She leaned up on an elbow, bringing her brows together in concern.

"What?"

"He had you practice using the souls in the poppy field?"

Lia laughed. "Yes."

The horror on Cal's face turned to shock and maybe disgust.

"Calm down, Calcas. I had the same reaction. He would never have let me harm a soul. If I pulled a soul from one poppy, it would move to rest in another. They are not tied to the flower. They only rest on it."

He pinched her side, causing her elbow to buckle as she laughed.

"You had me concerned you were out here damning souls for practice, little dragon."

"No, just a 300-year-old fae practicing her magic like a youngling."

The tone shift was audible. Cal reached down, lifting her chin to make her look into his eyes.

"Power isn't something you are born with, Lia, it's not the magic in your veins, it's born in the moments that call for strength when you have none."

The ship's hull scraped against the battered dock as mist clung to the air around them, obscuring most of Nightstone from view. The early morning sun had yet to burn it away, and it blurred everything to shades of gray.

Rayne was the first off the ship, talking to the guard on the dock, explaining who they were and also likely that the ship would shove off as soon as all four of them were off. Cal was in front of her eyes, scanning the surrounding fog like he expected something to jump out at any moment. In the distance, tower lights twinkled dully.

As was the plan, as soon as Aegaea stepped off the boat, the mooring lines were pulled and the boat moved away from the dock. Rayne would call for them when it was time for them to return.

Aegaea stepped up beside Lia. "It always smelled like something dies here."

Lia stared at the prison lights barely visible through the fog. "Something did, and the island keeps its bones."

"Cheerful." Aegaea laughed, moving to stand by her brother.

Lia stared out into the sea on the far side of the docks. The fog thinned over the water, but you still couldn't see much of anything but an expanse of cold blue. Just below the horizon was the only interruption in the sea. The outermost edge of the whirlpool was where the water just began to twist inward, slowly, deliberately.

She scanned the horizon, unable to find the beginning and edge of the disruption. The realization that it spanned the entire horizon line sank like a rock in her stomach. Bits of driftwood and seafoam were drawn to the edge before slipping away into the dark throat at its center.

She tore her eyes away and moved to the others, ready to be done with this shard.

"We made good time, the tide is already on its way in. We should be able to dive once we get ready," Rayne started as he began undressing. "Has Aegaea already explained how you'll breathe?"

Lia shook her head, the morning chill sinking into her bones, fusing with her anxiety and causing her bones to ache. Rayne motioned to Aegaea, drawing a dramatic eye roll from her as she finished folding the shirt in her hand and placing it on top of her boots. Her skin had already begun to shimmer as scales rose to the surface.

"It's just simple magic, we will maintain a pocket of air around your head so you can breathe. It's similar to the magic used to get to any of the sunken cities by ship, but on a smaller scale. On a normal trip, I could do both of you, but with everything else, it's safer to only have to breathe for one extra person each."

Cal gave a tight nod as he and Lia began undressing as well. He flashed Lia a small smirk when he caught her watching as he pulled his shirt over his head. She threw her boot at him, but he swiped it out of the air before it could make contact.

"Do we need to stay close to you?" Lia asked Aegaea, piling the last of her clothes together and shivering slightly as the fog dampened her exposed skin.

"For the magic, not really, just line of sight. But for the actual swim, you'll both have to hold onto us because you won't be able to make the dive well enough on your own. Not without fins."

Aegaea sat on the edge of the dock before gracefully slipping into the water. The transformation was instant. Her legs melded into a long tale, silver blue scales rippling down her form. Her nails and teeth elongated, gills tearing open along her throat and collarbone, and fins along her tail and arms glittered with barbed tips.

Rayne paused on the dock beside Cal with his hands on his hips, watching Aegaea dive for several minutes. She resurfaced, shaking her head.

"I don't see any immediate issues."

Lia heard Rayne let out a small breath. "Good. So we are diving straight here to the third ridge before we turn toward the whirlpool, right? Then, entering the flow at the spire height?"

Aegaea nodded from her place in the water, ripples moving out from her body in a slow pulse. "That should put us in the right position for the doors, from what I could tell. The doorway is wide and round, so we should enter easily. I don't know what to expect inside, but we won't have to fight the current once we are in."

Cal sucked his teeth sitting on the edge of the pier. "If we time it wrong—"

"We won't, Cal."

Lia was startled to find the words had come from her own lips, but she found she meant them. She trusted Aegaea. Cal watched her quietly before shrugging and turning back to the water just in time to get a face full of water as Rayne jumped in unceremoniously. His change was much the same as his sisters but his scales were a deep blue green.

Lia sat beside Cal, kissing him quickly before whispering, "Ready?"

"Never."

She smiled and slipped, feet first, into the frigid water.

Calcas

The water closed quickly over his head. He surfaced quickly, wiping the salt from his eyes. Rayne swam over to him, his bright smile plastered back on his warm features.

"I'm going to start giving you air, while we're under you won't be able to hear me or talk to me, so I need you to watch my face in case I need to tell you anything urgent." He placed a sharp, scaled hand on Cal's shoulder. "I need you to hold tight to me. If you need to get my attention, just squeeze my shoulder. As we get deeper, the pressure can be overwhelming, so I need you to focus on just holding onto me."

"Got it."

Cal looked over and found Lia talking quietly with Aegaea as she treaded water. He felt a cold burst of magic, the air around him buzzing. The next time Rayne spoke, it was dampened, like talking through a closed window.

"Let's go then."

Cal grabbed hold of Rayne's shoulders, watching Lia disappear beneath the surface with Aegaea. The water swallowed them whole. Below the surface, the water was cold and clear, and the pressure thickened as they descended into the dark gloom below. Rayne swam in tandem with Aegaea, slicing straight down the land mass of Nightstone, falling quickly away at their back.

The silence was otherworldly, nothing but his own rushed pulse and deep breaths filling the space around his ears. The little light from the surface slowly faded as they dove, clear water becoming smudgy blackness.

Rayne and Aegaea both glowed faintly in the darkness, their luminescent scales the only reason he could see anything at all. Out of the darkness, the sea floor loomed. Rayne leveled his body, swimming along the sand for a few moments before it dropped off dramatically, and they were diving again. They continued the silent descent, stopping on the edge of the third sandy outcropping they came upon. Aegaea and Rayne had an inaudible conversation, gesturing into the darkness and nodding.

Rayne tapped Cal's hand, drawing his attention. When they made eye contact, Rayne squeezed and mouthed, *hold tight*, before taking off into the darkness behind Aegaea and Lia. On the underwater ridge, the water had been cold and still. As they swam, warm currents began washing over Cal's skin, and the inky black began to lighten.

Out of the darkness, the whirlpool's form emerged. A monstrous cyclone, reaching toward the surface. The currents got stronger as they approached, but at this distance and depth they still weren't strong enough to draw them in. The form of the temple emerged as they approached. It was shaped similarly to the temple in Arachin, a single domed tower with an ornate spire.

The closer they swam to the temple, the more intense the currents became, twisting and pulling at them from all directions, and his grip tightened on Rayne's shoulder. The temple's massive stone structure rose from the sea floor like a forgotten God, its spire piercing upward through the dark waters. Faint glowing patterns ran along the walls that he couldn't fully make out through the roaring water.

Aegaea and Lia were already moving ahead, slicing through the current, the silvery glow of Aegaea's tail lighting their path. Lia's figure was barely visible behind the shimmering scales, but Cal could see her cling harder to Aegaea's small frame as they neared the violent water.

Cal's heartbeat thudded in his chest as the temple loomed closer. The whirlpool seemed to grow in size, an endless tunnel of rotating water that seemed all too eager to suck them in. They swam up slightly to use the natural current to enter the whirlpool as close as possible to the spire. With a few hard strokes, Cal felt the water around them change.

It drew them in as soon as they breached the outermost wall of the tempest. It dragged them around and down with immense force, circling the length of the tower, all the time, Rayne swimming across the current toward its eye wall. Finally, he saw the flicker of light he knew to be Aegaea disappear as it rounded the tower below them.

A dark, yawning mouth beneath a jagged arch of coral stained stone. The entrance was just below. The current carried them downward now with violent intent. As they reached the doorway, Rayne pushed hard, tearing through into the eye of the whirlpool, sending them careening into the mouth of the temple.

All around the small, dark chamber, symbols etched in deep green glowed faintly along the walls, pulsing like a heartbeat. Rayne swam upwards, and they broke the surface, emerging in a small grotto carved into the base of the temple. Slick stone steps led to a small, rough chamber lit with small flickering torches, where Lia and Aegaea now stood pulling on what looked like robes.

Cal pulled himself from the water, offering a hand to a panting Rayne as his transformation ran its course. Aegaea handed them both robes and dried Cal with her magic.

"There is a large stash of robes here, maybe for temple visitors in the past? They smell of damp and salt, but they will do for the hopefully short time we are here."

Rayne tied the belt of his robe, still panting slightly. "I *really* prefer to be on top of the water."

"You did seem to be slowing down a bit," Aegaea said, looking around the small chamber.

Elaborate carvings adorned the stone walls, depicting creatures he'd never seen before, serpentine beasts, their eyes carved in strange, unblinking detail.

Lia shivered slightly. "Do you know where you think the shard would be?"

"No," Aegaea shook her head. "I've never been in here before. I would assume that it's not in the main temple, though. I don't think the Salt Goddess knew what was here."

"It's nearly identical to Aduna's temple in Arachin from the outside," Cal said quietly.

Lia chewed her lip, pacing the small space.

"Down. We need to go down. We think one is under the temple there, and one was deep under the mountain. The magic burrows."

Lithia

The stone beneath her feet was slick with algae, and the air was thick with the smell of brine and stale air. Torchlight flickered off the damp walls, casting dancing shadows across the gently glowing carvings, serpents coiled through stylized waves, eyes of pearl and azure glinting in the low light, watching them pass.

Rayne kicked at a loose stone and gestured around. "Well, no stairs leading down in sight. More obviously, there aren't any doors or stairs leading upward either. I don't suppose one of these snake eyed carvings is secretly a door?"

"I wouldn't be surprised," Cal muttered, leaning close to one particularly large mosaic of a sea serpent. Its mouth hung open, rows of stone fangs glinting in the firelight. "In the mountain temple, there was a hidden door as well."

They fanned out across the chamber, each running soft hands over the stone. The faint pulse of magic vibrated through her bones like a distant heartbeat, deep and steady.

Lia moved toward the far wall, where a low basin had been carved into the rock. Faint traces of water puddled at the bottom. She reached down and attempted to dip her finger in. As her fingers brushed its surface, the water rippled, but there was resistance keeping her fingers from breaking the surface.

Aegaea joined her, eyes narrowed. "A ward," she said in a confused whisper.

Lia knelt at the base of a worn statue near the basin. "There's an inscription here. Faint, but it's still legible."

Rayne brought a torch over and squinted at the runes. "'The path below is sealed in sacrifice.'" He looked up at the others. "Not ominous at all."

"Could mean magic," Lia said quickly. "Or something symbolic."

"Could also mean blood," Cal added quietly, stepping up behind Lia.

Rayne leaned down to read the text again. As they all watched, the text shifted—letters slithered like eels through the stone, rearranging, pulsing faintly with greenish light, and a new message emerged, and Rayne read.

"Buried in lightless stone, where silence drowns sound, three twists will open the mouth."

He finished reading and barked out a laugh. "It's a puzzle box. It's not a temple, it's an enormous fucking puzzle box."

"Not a temple?" Lia asked, her mind struggling to keep up.

Aegaea sighed. "No, it is likely a temple as well, but the Salt Goddess was a fan of puzzles. Most Tidal fae are, the sea likes to hide many things, and so do we. I should have expected it."

Cal grunted behind her. "It took me nearly a year to open a puzzle box I won off Rayne, only to find my own cufflinks inside."

Rayne's grin was blinding. "Couldn't have you thinking you really beat me on my own ship. NOW," he said, turning quickly to the basin, "the simplest answer is usually the correct one."

Moving before she realized what he meant, Rayne had cut his palm with a small shell and was holding it over the bowl. As his blood hit the surface of the water in the bowl, the grinding sound of stone filled the room. On the wall beside them, the sea serpents moved, swimming in circles around each other, until the stone between them dissolved, revealing a dim curving passage.

They searched for hours.

Passages that looked promising dead ended into collapsed halls. Stairs led only to storage chambers, now filled with little more than coral and bones. In one chamber, an ancient altar held a waterlogged book, its pages long since rotted away, the cover etched with the Salt Goddess's broken trident.

Frustration clawed at her. The temple itself seemed determined to mislead. Paths shifted when they retraced their steps. Symbols they had passed before were suddenly rearranged or gone. Cal muttered curses under his breath when they opened the same cupboard a tenth time.

"It's like it's taunting us," he hissed.

"It is," Rayne said.

The temple was listening. Reacting.

"Then we need to figure out its language," Lia said.

She closed the door in front of them and looked around. They had opened every door and tried every set of steps they came to and gotten nowhere time and again. So she started walking. She walked straight down the passage, as it slowly curved upward. Not touching the doors. Never turning down the passages. Just pushed ahead with purpose, like she knew what lay at the end.

They walked in silence for several minutes before the passage stopped at a large door surrounded by the same pearl eyed serpents as the one they entered through. She pushed through the door and found a large circular chamber.

A great stone circle was carved into the floor, lined with jagged teeth of coral. Cal stepped around her to look closer, moving into the room. Light shimmered above it, forming a silvery mirage of the sea, moonlit and calm. Then, suddenly, the image shattered into violent waves, lightning crackling through the air. A voice vibrated like thunder through the clouds.

"Can you weather the storm?"

Without further warning, the stone beneath their feet dropped away.

She landed in...water? Real water. Somehow, impossibly, she was submerged, her limbs scrambling for purchase in the sudden cold as waves crashed over her. A storm raged in every direction, disorienting and endless. But this wasn't real—it couldn't be. She forced herself to be still, to center her breath.

She breathed deeply before she sank into the water, the sound of the storm above muting as the water closed over her head. She floated downward for several seconds before her feet landed on the solid stone of the floor. She opened her eyes, and the storm was gone. Aegaea dried them all from where she sat on the other side of the circle.

"I guess it just wanted us to wait?" she said, her melodic voice sounded tired.

"Whatever it wanted, it got it because there's a new door." Cal sounded like he would rather have had to fight his way to the shard than endure this, and Lia was inclined to agree.

They moved through the door and followed the new passage for several minutes until it deposited them in another circular room with three statues at its center. Three blindfolded Tidal fae holding shallow bowls, each facing a different direction. Above the first was a small trickle of water falling directly into her bowl, then cascading out the side.

Moving closer to inspect them, Cal pointed out a divot in the floor beside the third statue.

"I assume we need to get that water into this hole?"

Rayne gnawed his lip as he stooped to inspect the base of the third statue, pushing on it gently.

"Do they mo—"

A soft grinding sound as the statue before him rotated a quarter turn. He looked up with a triumphant smile that fell as soon as he saw the look on Lia and Aegaea's faces.

"They all turned," Lia explained quickly.

His nose wrinkled as he straightened and watched all three statues as he pushed on the third again. They all turned at different rates, the first doing a half rotation, the second half that, and the last half of the second. He pushed it again...and again...and again...

They watched as Rayne slowly rotated the statues over and over with a winkle of concentration forming between his brows. Over an hour later, with one final push, they slipped into place. The water cascaded from one to the next, pouring gently into the small divot in the floor.

As they watched the next door form on the floor, revealing a slow spiraling set of stairs, Cal clapped Rayne on the shoulder.

"Do you think you could have just used your magic to move the water to the lock?"

Rayne's face fell, and Aegaea spoke, "No, I tried it after the first few minutes, it didn't respond to me."

"I can't believe you didn't trust me," came her brother's indignant reply as he pushed Cal and started for the door.

LITHIA

T he last puzzle was the worst.

They had followed the stairs in an endless downward spiral before being spat out in front of a solid wall. It wasn't a chamber. Just a mirror of obsidian. When Lia stepped up to it, her reflection met her, but it didn't move with her.

It smiled.

It whispered.

Words meant only for her. Words from the deepest part of her soul. Her fears. She stood, frozen, while the voice tried to unmake her.

"You are the broken thing. You are the wound. You, Lithia, are the rot. The void."

She nearly shattered beneath it.

She thought of the love in Cal's eyes when he looked at her. She thought of Neda losing half of herself and staying to fight. She thought of the visible pain etched on Tadhg's body, never dulling the happiness he shares with everyone. She thought of Wil sharing her deepest truths for any hope of saving them all.

She faced herself in the mirror as her magic burst from her skin, shattering it, turning it to dust. *"I am the bridge. Not the break."*

The chamber beyond the shattered mirror pulsed with a green tinged glow, as if moonlight was filtered through the sea. The air was heavy with the weight of ancient magic. At the room's center, resting atop a pedestal of spiraled coral and stone, was the shard of tidal magic.

It hovered just above the pedestal, a translucent sliver of sea glass that shimmered with blues, greens, and the occasional flicker of lightning. The surrounding walls bore murals of the Salt Goddess in various forms—stormbringer, tidecaller, deep dweller. All watching. All waiting.

Lia approached, her bare feet whispering across the wet stone. Her heart thrummed in rhythm with the shard's energy, like waves crashing in her chest.

She reached out.

As her fingers brushed the shard, the world inverted.

Water surged around her, though she wasn't drowning. She stood at the bottom of the sea, darkness pressing in, anchoring her in the silence. Magic, immense and resonant, rolled through the water, a siren song echoing in her mind.

The shard dissolved into a burst of blinding blue light, then plunged into her chest like a blade of cold water. She gasped, staggering backward into the real world as her body arched, her runes glowing with blue fire.

Then, silence.

The room dimmed.

Lia collapsed to her knees, gasping. Cal caught her just before she fell face first into the stone. Her body was on fire with boiling magic and salt burns.

Cal held her to his chest. "How do you feel?"

Lia blinked the blur from her eyes. "Like I've swallowed the ocean."

The temple rumbled.

"Time to go," Rayne said quickly, glancing up as debris fell from the ceiling.

Cal supported Lia as they made their way back to the entrance.

They wove through the corridors that had misled them, the path now clear. The temple no longer taunted them. It was finished.

But the sea was not.

They emerged into the small grotto to find fog curled across the water's surface, the water spilling over the steps.

Aegaea began pulling off her robe as she spoke. "We should be able to exit the cyclone easier than entering, we don't have to aim anywhere but out. Let's be quick about it, though we didn't—"

Then the water erupted.

Formed from the water, four necsite rose from the water's surface in their demon form.

"They weren't here when we arrived, but they must have felt the magic," Cal said in a quiet voice.

An ear-splitting wail bounced off the bare walls in a cacophony of noise. The largest of the four shifted grotesquely between demon and horse, body slick with brine and rot.

They surged.

Rayne spun forward, sending daggers of ice into the nearest creature, black blood mixing with water. Aegaea raised her hands, creating a wall of water between them and the oncoming attack.

Lia didn't flinch.

She breathed deeply, pushing her fear down deep, and reached for their magic. One by one. She found the magical threads that seared her mouth with ash and tar.

She wrapped her syphon around them all at once, inhaled, and pulled.

The magic slipped from their cores with ease. She could taste the decay of the void magic where it had already begun to break down the fibers of their magic. She pulled the magic from them, their life force slipping away with it. The water exploded with the force of the magic, flooding the room.

Rayne looked at her in shock. "That was terrifying."

"It most certainly was, little dragon," Cal said, wonder in his eyes.

Lia smiled weakly at them both, fighting the urge to collapse again.

"Let's get out of here before the sea asks for something in return."

CALCAS

Cal broke the surface, the cold brine clinging to his lungs. Every muscle burned from the pressure of the long, slow ascent from the whirlpool's grasp to the surface. The water here pulsed with the usual ebb and flow of the sea, the violent pull of the whirlpool far in the distance.

Rayne bobbed in the water beside him, breathing heavily, hair slicked back, rubbing at the muscles in his shoulder. A moment later, Lia came up, nearly limp, barely able to keep herself above the surface as Aegaea kept her afloat. Her eyes were wide and unfocused, and even though she was breathing, Cal felt something sharp twist in his chest.

They swam in silence toward the edge of Nightstone and the relief of the docks. Cal reached them first and hauled himself up with a groan, then turned to help Rayne pull Lia from the sea. Her limbs were stiff, but she murmured something unintelligible as he hoisted her from the water.

He held her tightly, arms locked beneath her knees and around her shoulders, careful not to jostle her too much as he carried her across the slick wood to where their dry clothes were waiting. Below the horizon, Rayne's ship barreled toward them, whitecapped spray at the hull as it made its way toward the island.

Rayne or Aegaea dried them. He didn't see who as he gently helped Lia into her clothes before dressing himself. By the time he was pulling Lia back into his lap, the ship was being tied off, and Rayne was greeting his men. He stood, curling Lia into his chest, and climbed onboard, Aegaea gently touching his arm as he passed, taking Lia into the cabins to sleep.

The ship eased back into motion with the wind's soft pull. Rayne took the wheel, barking hoarse orders that faded with each step he took. The sails caught with a cracking snap as they began moving toward the port at Fernholme.

Cal stood at the rail, gripping the damp wood tight enough to splinter it. The salt air cut through him like ice, but his thoughts stayed fixed below deck. Lia had only slept a short time before she woke screaming. Once she had finally calmed, she had pushed him from the room.

She hadn't said a word to him.

She hadn't even *looked* at him.

He found her again hours later, curled in a corner of their narrow bed, a worn blanket around her shoulders, with Aegaea kneeling by her hands, softly braiding her hair where it had dried in tangled waves down her back.

"She hasn't slept again," Aegaea said quietly when she saw him at the door. "Won't eat. Won't talk. I don't know if it's pain, or pride, or both."

She slipped quietly out the door, leaving him alone with Lia once more.

Cal stepped in, crouching beside Lia, his voice low. "What is it?"

She didn't answer. Her eyes remained fixed on the far wall, lashes fluttering with each shallow breath.

"Lia." He reached out, gently brushing his fingers against her temple. Her skin was ice.

She flinched away, her whole body stiffening as she curled tighter into herself.

"You're freezing. You need —"

"It's just the magic," she said, voice barely a whisper, but her jaw locked tight.

"This isn't just the magic, little dragon," he sighed. "You *ripped* the magic out of four necsites, but that was *your* magic, and you have much better control of it. What else is going on?"

"I *said* I'm fine."

"Look at me, dragon."

Silence stretched between them.

She didn't turn. She didn't speak.

Cal exhaled hard through his nose, fighting to keep the heat out of his voice. "You don't have to protect yourself from me, Lia."

Her eyes finally flicked toward him, narrowed and sharp. "I'm not protecting *me*. I'm protecting all of you from *me*."

"What in the Goddess's tits is that supposed to mean?"

She stood too fast, swaying on her feet as she leaned against the wall. Cal reached out to steady her, but Lia waved him off. Her breath hitched, and Cal saw it just before the pain hit her full force. She staggered, both hands flying to her head like it was splitting open from the inside.

Cal lunged forward and caught her before she fell.

"Stop," she whispered into his neck, her voice brittle. "Please—don't make me explain. I can't."

He held her tight, ignoring the way she trembled in his arms. "You don't get to fall apart in my hands and then pretend you're fine. We are so far past this, Lia."

"I *have* to pretend," she whispered, her voice shaking. "Because if I don't, she wins."

He pulled back just enough to see her face. Her eyes were rimmed in red beneath the salty curls on her brow that had stayed free of her braid.

"What's she doing to you?" he asked, forcing the rising anger back down his throat.

Lia hesitated.

Then, finally, she spoke, voice low and cracking. "I don't know, Cal, but I'm unraveling."

The blood in his veins chilled.

"I *will* fight for you," he said. "Even if it means dragging you back from the edge, kicking and screaming."

She looked away, and Cal watched the walls go back up behind her eyes. She scooted off his lap, curling back onto the narrow bed.

He kissed her softly.

"Get some rest," he said quietly. "Anything that wants you has to go through me first."

As he stood and turned for the stairs, he heard her whisper behind him before the door clicked shut.

"That's what I'm afraid of."

He stayed on the deck until the moon rose high over the sea, silver and watchful. They sailed quickly and quietly through the night, but Cal's stomach never settled.

They were almost to Fernholme, one step closer to the next piece of this God sized puzzle. But for the first time, Cal wasn't sure if they were gaining ground—or if the universe was just letting them think they were before it tore them apart.

LITHIA

The dream didn't begin in darkness.

It began in light, blinding, golden, and warm, like the first breath of summer after a long, cruel winter. Lia blinked against the brilliance, her breath catching in her throat as her bare feet brushed soft, dew drenched grass. The scent of salt and honeysuckle filled the air, familiar and foreign all at once.

Birdsong drifted lazily across the horizon. Somewhere in the distance, a youngling laughed.

Lia turned slowly in place, her eyes scanning the sun-drenched field. Rolling hills arced into the distance, crowned with wildflowers that sparkled like stars. A lake shimmered beyond the slope, as still and smooth as polished glass.

Someone stood at the edge.

Cal.

He smiled the kind of unguarded smile he hadn't worn in years.

"Lia," he said, his voice distant.

Her heart surged painfully. She ran to him without thought.

He caught her, strong arms wrapping around her waist, lifting her slightly off the ground as her face buried in the crook of his neck. She smelled the smoke on his skin. Heard the whispered thud of his heartbeat against her cheek.

"I missed you," she breathed, voice breaking.

"You don't have to miss it anymore," he murmured. "We're here now, together, and nothing can take it away."

*But even as he said it, something **shifted**.*

A cold wind whipped around her, sharp and wrong. The light dimmed. The scent of honeysuckle soured, tinged with iron. Lia pulled back. The hills trembled at the edges. The sky warped, and the lake began to ripple.

"Cal?" she whispered.

His smile didn't fade, but it froze, like it was painted on.

A voice like honey rose all around her.

"This is what could be, Lithia. All you need to do is trust me. Help me fix everything."

The meadow had gone still, and Cal faded in front of her. Lia turned. At the center of it all stood Seren, radiant in a gown of black silk that slipped like ink down her body. Her gold eyes measured Lia in the silence, sharper than the oversweet tone of her voice.

The illusion remade itself further.

The grass flattened into polished marble, veined in silver. The sky above grew darker, like twilight bleeding into the clouds.

Lia stepped back.

"What is this?" she asked, her voice thick with dread.

Seren tilted her head, as if Lia had missed something.

"This is the world I can give you."

Seren moved closer, her bare feet silent on the stone. Around her, shadowy figures began to appear in the periphery, familiar faces. Her mother, her father, Narcos, more faces than she could make out in detail. All of them smiling, whole.

Alive.

"The veil is not sacred," *Seren whispered.* **"It was never meant to exist. It was built to punish a God, and in doing so, it tore our realms in two. But if we bring it down, the Beneath will return to Suviel. Death will no longer be the end. And you, Cal, me...we can all live again. Together."**

Lia felt her eyes burn, "You're lying," Lia rasped, though even as she said it, her resolve faltered.

"Am I?"

Seren turned and gestured to the horizon.

The vision shifted again.

They stood atop a cliff, overlooking Suviel. But it was whole. Fields stretched green and gold across the plains. The fields shimmered with healthy growth. The sky was unmarred by storm or fire, and in the distance, cities gleamed like polished jewels.

But more than that—she could feel them.

The souls.

Walking alongside the living. No torment, no wailing. Simply... being. Ancestors. Children lost too soon. Lovers reunited. A world without endings.

"Isn't this what you've always wanted?"** Seren asked softly. **"To save everyone. To stop losing the people you love. To stop breaking apart every time fate decides you've had enough happiness."

Lia's knees gave out beneath her. She collapsed onto the smooth stone, her breath shallow.

"I'm trying to hold them together," she whispered. "The shards... I'm trying..."

Seren knelt before her. "But they're not yours to hold, little dragon."

And as if the words summoned it, the surge hit her.

Lia screamed.

Blue white magic erupted from her chest, cracking her ribs outward like a cage trying to shatter. Her veins ignited with fire. She clutched at her chest, but the magic writhed beneath her skin.

"You're unraveling," Seren said, calm amid chaos. *"Because you're trying to contain something meant to be released."*

Lia gasped, curling in on herself as another violent surge tore through her spine. The ground beneath her shattered, silver cracks racing out from where her hands touched.

"You don't have to suffer. You don't have to fight anymore. Say yes. Let me finish what has already begun."

A final wave of agony overtook her. Her mouth opened in a wordless scream, light pouring from her throat, her fingertips splitting open with raw magic. Her body began to fracture like glass under a hammer.

And Seren stood over her, smiling, waiting.

"Say yes."

Lia choked on her answer.

Through the blinding pain, the screams in her head, and the bastardized visions of peace, she forced out the word.

"Never."

She woke with a *gasp*, a scream ripped from her lungs as if drowning in air.

The room erupted around her.

Blue fire crackled out of her skin in surging arcs, dancing up the walls and ripping through the floorboards. The bed split beneath her. Books, weapons, clothes, lifted from their shelves, suspended in the air, caught in a storm of power.

The small table exploded into splinters.

The door slammed open.

"LIA!" Cal's voice, ragged with fear.

He didn't hesitate. He crossed the room in two strides, only to be thrown back by a blast of magic that flung him across the cabin. Aegaea scrambled in behind him, barely shielding herself in time as another wave of wild power tore through the space.

Lia arched off the bed, eyes glowing. Magic pouring from her mouth, her fingertips, her spine. Her veins pulsed with swirling magic.

Cal crawled toward the bed, bruised and bleeding, teeth clenched against the pressure in the air.

"Lia—"

"She's inside me!" Lia screamed. *"I see her when I sleep. I hear what she wants!"*

Her limbs jerked violently, spasming. One of her legs kicked back and cracked the bedframe. Her hands clawed at her own arms, tearing at them in fear.

Cal caught her at last, grabbing her wrists and pulling her into his lap as the storm began to collapse inward. She trembled violently in his grasp.

"Then don't let her win," he whispered into her hair, tightening his grip on her.

The light in her eyes blazed, then she felt it snap, leaving an empty hum in its wake. Lia collapsed, her breathing shallow but steady, the storm fizzing out into soft, static sparks dancing across her skin. Cal held her, rocking slowly as Aegaea nodded, backing quickly out of the room.

He kissed Lia's brow, voice barely audible.

"I've got you."

CALCAS

The gulls circled the port at Fernholme, their cries piercing the exhausted silence as they disembarked. Cal leaned against a crate, the wind tugging strands free of his topknot to fly in his face, salt stinging his dry lips. He didn't bother to fix either issue. His mind wasn't really there, as he watched the hearth sentinels crowd the dock with Nylian's arrival.

Lithia stood leaning into his side slightly, the last few days heavy on her shoulders. They were exhausted, all of them, in different ways. Unfortunately, Cal's current exhaustion had a name.

Seren.

He hadn't told the others. Not yet. Hadn't told them about the shadowed letter that floated across the moonlit deck to him the night before they entered the whirlpool. The single line swam through his mind on an endless loop. The guilt at not telling Lithia burned like poison in his stomach.

The temple at Fernholme on the night you arrive.

The castle was quieter than he remembered when they entered. It had always smelled like rosewood and soil, something sweet and alive. The Prime's castle was a place of relentless order and precision, but most of all whispers. But today, it felt quietly watchful. As if the very walls had sensed what was coming and decided to wait it out in silence.

They were escorted up the steps, wet boots leaving dark prints on the soft wood floors. Wil and Neda met them halfway up the main stairs, joining the slow parade toward their rooms. The vast hall glowed with filtered sunlight through stained glass, casting golden vines across the walls and floors. Neda's sleeves were rolled to her elbows, hair tied back in a messy knot, a faint streak of charcoal across her cheek.

"You've found something?" Lia asked quietly.

"I found *too* many somethings." She gestured vaguely. "I'll take you to the tree in the morning after you've all gotten to rest some."

They began splitting off into their rooms.

Rayne, who was already loosening his belts with an audible sigh as he pushed his door open, muttered, "Tell me they have baths."

Neda stopped behind him and laughed softly. "Why wouldn't we have baths?"

"You'd be surprised at the places I've stayed," he said with a wink as he closed the door.

Cal followed Lia into their room, shaking his head, ready to sleep on solid ground.

He wasn't sure when his feet had begun moving.

The city was quiet beneath moonlight, the glow from the city gates turning the vine woven walls of Fernholme into something almost sinister, like bone. Cal's boots made no sound against the dusty street, and the guards had no reason to question him as plenty of taverns were still open and crawling with lively fae.

He told himself it was for air.

For clarity.

For the distance from the heaviness.

But it wasn't any of those things.

Not really.

He reached a door with the half-burnt sigil above it, a deeply overgrown temple. The reverence of this place was deeply rooted in the soil. It was quiet and empty at this time of night.

Seren stood at the edge of the altar, her hands folded loosely before her as if she had all the time in the world. His shadows curled out, reaching for her, pooling at her feet. Her black leathers shone in the low torchlight, her glinting helm sat behind her on the altar, making Cal's skin crawl.

"Calcas," she said, as though tasting the word. "You came."

"I shouldn't have."

But he didn't move.

Seren tilted her head. "Yet here you are."

Cal took a breath, slow and controlled, but his lungs were tight. "If you wanted to kill me, you would've. If you wanted Lia, you would've tried again while she was unconscious," he growled. "So what do you want?"

Seren stepped around the altar, her booted steps soundless. "Mmm, killing you would be wasteful. And I've grown tired of waste."

She circled him like smoke, her fingers trailing lightly along the altar as she walked. "You love her," she said, and there was something razor edged in the way she said *love*, like it didn't fit in her mouth. "You want her to live. To be happy. To be free."

Cal didn't answer.

"I do, too," Seren continued. "But what you fail to understand is that this mission you're on, it will *never be enough.*"

A muscle in his jaw ticked, but he bit back his response and let her talk.

"All she's doing is ripping herself apart," Seren said softly. "Did you see her after she took that shard into herself?" *She laughed.* "Of course you did. You *held* her. You smelled the salt burns on her skin. You heard the silence afterward, the kind that only follows something *wrong.*"

Cal flinched despite himself.

"You think she can carry all of it?" Seren asked, stepping toward him. "Do you think she was *built* for this? She wasn't. None of you were."

"We don't have a choice."

Seren's eyes gleamed, catching the flickering light like twin gold coins. "But you *do.*"

She stepped even closer, and now she was within arm's reach. He could see the faint glow of the fire in her eyes.

"I want the same thing you do," she said, softer now. "I want *all* of you to live. There is only one way to fix this without killing her in the process, Calcas."

He didn't stop her when she touched his chest, right over his heart.

"Help me shatter the veil."

He growled. "No."

She whispered, "The veil is a wound, not a gift. It was a punishment crafted by terrified Gods who didn't understand what they were doing. Death was *never* meant to be a cage."

"And what?" Cal said, voice rising. "You'll break it open and just hope the monsters don't come too?"

"They're *already* here," Seren snapped, sudden and sharp. "You've fought them. You've watched them slither through the world living their lives."

She stepped back, letting her voice cool again. "But if the veil falls *on our terms,* we control the way it breaks. We bring back what was lost."

Cal's throat worked, but no words came.

She saw it. The hesitation. And pounced.

"You could bring your father back."

He froze.

Seren murmured close to his ear. "I remember the way you screamed when your father didn't wake. But you don't have to carry his ghost anymore. You could speak to him again. You could *have* him again."

His heart pounded. He could hear it over the sound of his breath.

"Peace," she said. "For Lia. For you. For everyone."

He stared at her.

A choice.

A trap.

"If we fail," Seren whispered, stepping close again, "if Lia *dies,* then all this struggle will have been for *nothing.* But if we work together, *no one has to die at all.*"

She stepped back. "This choice *is* yours, truly. But if you love her—and I know you do—*don't be the reason she dies.*"

Cal didn't speak, just turned on his heel and walked away.

He didn't look back. Not even when she said softly, almost lovingly, *"You'll know when the moment comes."*

The alcove outside his and Lia's quarters was small and quiet as he slid off his boots. The moment the door shut behind him, the mask dropped from Cal's face, and he sighed, curling in on himself.

"You went to her," Wil's sharp tone raked down his spine.

He turned towards the direction of the accusation and found Wil sitting in the straight backed chair in the corner, covered in shadow, her hands digging grooves into the dark wood. He ran his hand down his face, swallowing the lump in his throat.

"She found me," Cal said, defeated.

"No, Calcas, she called you like a dog and you came."

"I needed answers."

"Seeking those from Seren was reckless."

"I needed to know if Lia would survive it, Wil." His voice cracked. "She's coming apart. I saw it. You weren't there. I—" Cal's breath hitched. "If she reforges the heart, there's a chance it might kill her. Seren said—"

"Seren says *many* things," Wil bit out, standing. "And you of all people should know, she *never* says anything without knowing the cost."

Cal's jaw tightened, but he didn't reply.

"She's clawing her way into Lia's *mind,* Cal. She's using every ounce of Lia's doubt and love against her. And now she's doing it to *you.* You need to be stronger than she thinks you are."

"She's not—"

"She *is,*" Wil snapped. "I saw the way she looked at you when you left. Like she *knew* she didn't have to touch you to break you."

The silence between them stretched.

Then—

"I don't want to lose her," Cal whispered.

Wil's voice softened. "Then don't make it easier for Seren to take her."

A movement behind him.

Both turned.

Lia stood in the doorway to their room.

Her skin was pale, her eyes bright with fury.

"You already *are,*" she said with a hiss.

Cal turned toward her, horror etching his features. "Lia—"

"You went to her. *You let her in.*" Lithia's voice was low and lethal.

"It wasn't like that—"

"Then *what* was it like?" she asked, louder now. "Because the only thing worse than someone trying to destroy me is my mate helping her do it."

Wil took a step forward, sensing the impending storm, but was stopped by Lia's hand.

Cal stepped forward. "Lia, I thought I was doing it for *you*. I didn't want to risk—"

"It's already a risk. It's *always* a risk!" she shouted. "You think I don't know that? That I don't feel her every time I close my eyes? That I don't hear her whispering *what if it's all for nothing?*" Her breath hitched, but she kept going. "I *trusted* you to believe in me when I couldn't believe in myself."

Cal felt himself shatter as he reached for her. "Lia—please—"

She stepped back. Just one step. But it said everything.

"You have to choose," she said, voice cracking. "Now."

The castle around them held its breath.

Cal's lips parted.

And nothing came out.

Lia turned and walked away.

LITHIA

L ithia didn't speak the entire walk from the castle to the grove.

The stone pavers beneath her boots were wet with morning dew, and the canopy above them glittered with floating lights woven between tree branches with spider silk, thin threads of magic. Fernholme always breathed like it was half asleep, like something old and wild lived beneath its roots and didn't care for time as any on the surface understood it.

Cal walked a few paces behind her.

She couldn't look at him.

She could feel the weight of his gaze, could feel the guilt clinging to him like damp clothing, but she couldn't bring herself to meet it. Not yet. Not when her chest still felt hollow from the crack that had formed the moment he hesitated.

"Just beyond here," Neda said tiredly, drawing their attention from its downward spiral.

The grove opened slowly before them, a cathedral of light and green. Tall, ancient trees formed a circle around the Tree of Beginnings. The air shimmered faintly with old enchantments and wards. Roots coiled through the soil like sleeping serpents, flowers blooming from their knots in vivid colors, painting the ground.

The tree at the center was enormous, like the three in the Singing Wood. Its trunk twisted up and up until it disappeared into the canopy, branches dripping with silver leaves that caught the sun like mirrors. Its bark pulsed faintly, like a heartbeat, and Lithia's magic buzzed in her fingertips the moment she stepped into the glade.

"It *is* here."

She knew it. She could feel the shard thrumming from the ancient tree. Her lungs tightened as she stared at it, beautiful, terrible.

Neda stepped forward and knelt, brushing her fingers across the moss that encircled the tree's roots.

"So, we have to figure out how to get to it still."

Lithia stared at the tree, the image of its twin in the Singing Wood filling her mind, and she smiled.

"No, I thin—"

From the edges of the grove, they stepped out of the trees. Fae. Dozens of them. Silent. Their armor gleamed, gold and green, patterned with leaves and thorns. Their expressions were cold, not hostile, but not welcoming.

A tall fae stepped forward from among them, face half hidden beneath a veil of ivy. Her skin shimmered like sunlight through canopy leaves. Her voice, when she spoke, was like iron.

"Lithia Caileanach, High Queen of the Fae, Prime of Suviel, Daughter of Mab," each title sank like a stone, "you are not welcome here. I'm sorry, *Mo Bhanrighit.*"

The others behind her did not raise their weapons, but their stance shifted. Cal tensed beside her. She could feel it, the way his shadows curled out to meet her, ready to unfurl at a breath. But she raised a finger to stop him.

Neda stepped between them and the fae. "They were given permission by the prime, and Mab's line has never been denied access to the grove. Stand down."

"Her magic is unstable," the fae countered. "The void grows wider *in* her. Narcos is dead, and her shadow stretches long beyond his fall. She is not only dangerous, she is the source of much of this."

Lithia flinched.

Cal stepped forward. "If she's breaking, it's because of what she's had to carry. What she's *still* carrying. To save us all."

The fae woman's eyes flicked to him, cool and unimpressed. "She is failing."

"You will not spe—"

Lithia's breath hitched. "Stop."

The wind died.

"I do not need your permission," she said. Her voice was low, steady. "I came because the world is unraveling, and it is mine to save or die trying. We don't have the time to argue over who has the right to try and save it."

A long silence passed. Then the woman stepped aside.

"We will not help you," she said. "But we will not stop you either."

Lithia stepped forward.

The grove fell into stillness.

Each step toward the tree felt like walking through a thousand years of memory as the tree clung to her footsteps. The closer she drew, the louder her pulse became in her ears. Her breath came shallow. The magic stilled like the tree was holding its breath.

She reached the base of the tree and laid her hand against the bark.

It was warm, alive.

Images flickered through her mind, from eyes that were not her own. The forming of the veil. The fracture of the shards. The first heartbeats of hearth. She saw the forest. When she touched this tree's brother.

But this time...

This time was different.

The bark shuddered beneath her touch. A seam split down the center of the trunk, glowing with golden light. She felt the shard's power move toward her, like a river parting around stone.

She held still, pressing her palm more firmly into the bark.

It floated out of the trunk, a glowing fragment of amber, warm and flickering. As it touched her palm, the world seemed to pause.

There was no pain.

There was only...warmth.

The magic seeped into her gently, like fingers combing through her hair, like a heartbeat slipping in time with her own. It filled her veins like sunlight. The fear that usually followed, the shattering, the tearing, the burn, never came. It *belonged*. For the first time, it didn't fight her. Lithia exhaled.

The light dimmed. The tree closed once more, and the shard was gone, a part of her now. She turned slowly, her eyes catching Cal's. His mouth was parted slightly, something like awe softening his expression.

A ripple of magic pulsed across the glade as a shadow crossed the sky. The grove held its breath a final time as a figure stepped through the arch of trees. *Seren.* She looked unbothered. Her opaline armor shimmered in the sunlight.

A feral grin split her face.

"Well done, my love," she said, words tainted like spoiled fruit.

Cal's morningstar was in his hand before anyone blinked. "You shouldn't be here."

"I go where I please," Seren said smoothly, her eyes never leaving Lia. "Besides, I came to offer a choice."

"No," Lithia said.

"Please, some haven't even heard it yet," Seren purred.

"And they don't need to," she snapped.

Seren's face darkened. "Pity. I'd hoped you could be civil."

She raised a hand, and magic exploded across the grove.

The hearth fae raised their defenses instantly, shields of light snapping up in overlapping domes. Cal stepped in front of Lithia, shadows lashing out to meet Seren's magic. Neda and Wil flanked them, blades drawn.

Lithia stepped around them, drawing Mab's sword.

The grove broke open.

CALCAS

The moment Lithia moved, the world narrowed.

No battle cry. No warning.

Just motion, furious and absolute, as her blade left its sheath and erupted with swirling galaxies of magic. She didn't wait for the others. Didn't wait for him. She surged forward, wings tearing from her back.

And all Cal could do was follow wherever she led.

His stride hit the roots with force as he sprinted after her, his morningstar spinning low and heavy in his hand. The grove's soil was thick with roots of the Tree of Beginnings as it groaned as if mourning what was to come.

Then the darkness came.

Seren's magic hit without warning, a wall of unraveling blackness. It wasn't shadow. It wasn't fire or water or any element Cal understood. It was an absence. A darkness that didn't just obscure it unmade the world around it.

Screams rang through the grove as fae were flung back, limp, their armor collapsing and shields faltering. At the center of it all stood Seren, her true face revealed, every inch a mask of death and ruin. Her eyes were empty sockets of starless black. Her hair floated as if underwater, tangled with thorns and mist. Her skin was rotting from her bones, and her magic writhed like a living thing as it devoured everything around her.

Cal felt his soul shrink from her.

But something else flared within him. *Rage.* There had never really been a choice to make. He raised his hand. The shadows answered, surging up from the roots. They wrapped around his arms, curled beneath his skin, and hummed along his magic. He invited them.

And they came.

A wall of shadow bloomed between Seren's spell and the line of hearth fae, soft at first, then solid like iron. Her magic slammed into it, splintering like glass against velvet.

He turned his head and found her, Lithia, already cutting through one of the newly arrived Hunt. Her sword, now burned with a strange shimmer of green gold, flickering magic that rolled up the blade like waves.

She was brilliant.

But she was alone.

"Lia!" he shouted over the roar.

She turned. Her braid snapped around her eyes, locking on his. She grinned as his shadows rolled across the roots toward her. She steeled her spine, swinging on the wraith in front of her again. The magic rolling on her sword darkened into rolling waves of shadow and flame.

And Cal *felt* it.

She wielded it with elegance and fury. Where his magic craved stillness, hers was never ending movement. Where his shadow suffocated, hers cut.

Lithia ran toward Seren, sword raised.

"You have no power over me," she whispered.

And then she moved.

Cal was at her side a breath later, his morningstar catching a blade mid swing, the collision cracking like thunder. He whirled low, the iron ball tearing through one of the wraiths, aiming for Lia as she attacked Seren.

Seren's laughter was sharp and mocking.

"You think this is a *victory?*" she sneered, her voice echoing in a dozen broken tones. "This is a prelude to ruin."

Seren moved like lightning—a spike of black glass burst from her palm, flying for Lithia's chest. Shadow roared from him, catching the spike inches from her heart. He dissolved it into dust. To his shock, Lithia didn't even blink. She *trusted* him. And his heart panged because he wasn't sure he had earned that.

They fought in a rhythm. When Cal blocked high, she struck low. When she overextended, his shadows curled around her waist and held her in balance.

They didn't speak. They didn't need to.

But around them, the grove was in chaos.

Wil and Neda held off several wraiths near the edge of the grove, barely keeping Seren's twisted magic from consuming them. Neda bled from her thigh but still shouted orders, holding a line that should've crumbled long ago. Leaves from the Tree of Beginnings fell around them, in a shower of green.

Seren raised her arms, and the sky turned black. She screamed and charged, and it echoed like the scream of something ancient and dying. The roots around the grove snapped upward, writhing. Shadows coiled through the air, and suddenly the tree itself shuddered.

His morningstar spun. It caught her blade once...

Twice...

Then was flung wide.

She nearly reached him, but Lithia was there, sword catching Seren's next strike.

Sparks flew.

Seren hissed at her. "I believed in *saving* it. I wanted to pull the world together, Lia. Now all I want is to shred it with my bare hands."

Lithia didn't answer. Her eyes flared, and her sword, his shadow curling around its flame, cut a streak across Seren's side.

Seren staggered.

"You will not survive this," she snarled and backed away several steps. "But I will."

And she was gone.

Cal turned to Lithia and saw her standing there, blood on her face, sword digging into the soil, lowered but not yet sheathed. Her hands shook. Her jaw trembled. But she was alive.

He stepped into her, "Are you alright, little dragon?"

She laughed once, bitter and breathless. "I think I might be sick."

"Go ahead, just give me a second."

He wrapped his hand softly around her neck and pulled her into a slow kiss, pouring the guilt and apologies into it. She kissed him back fiercely before pulling back to look at him. There was a recognition in her expression that made his heart stutter with relief.

LITHIA

Ash drifted where leaves once shimmered. The roots of the Tree of Beginnings curled inward as if in pain, bruised from the magic and blood. The wards etched into the stones were flat and dull, flickering. Whatever serenity the place had held was broken, replaced by the weight of something wounded and fragile, but it would heal.

Lithia stood in the center of it all, the magic humming quietly in her chest. The magic had settled some, but the rest of her hadn't, and she needed an outlet.

Across the grove, Cal helped a wounded hearth fae to their feet. Neda and Wil were already coordinating with the others, as Tadhg began healing some of the more gravely wounded. The last of The Hunt had fled with Seren, vanishing as swiftly and silently as they'd arrived.

Lithia knelt briefly by the tree, placing her palm against its bark again. A pulse of magic met her, weak, but still present. Behind her, Cal approached, his footfalls light. His shadows reached for her, curling softly around her. She stood and turned to face him, taking him in fully. His armor was scorched. His upper lip was split. There was a thin line of blood beneath one eye. He moved a piece of hair off one cheek before kissing her lightly on the forehead and gesturing to where Neda and Wil stood.

Wil spoke as they approached, "We should rest. I didn't expect us to find this shard so easily, but everything else was even less expected."

Lia shook her head. "No, we need to make a plan and leave for Dragos soon to get the next shard. We can't waste time."

Cal sighed. "I agree with Wil. I don't think the rest is wasting time, Lia. You are taking on this magic quickly, and I'm worried that if we move too quickly, you'll collapse in on yourself."

"Fine, but we still meet tonight to make a plan."

They all nodded before Lia turned on her heel and made her way to her chambers.

Cal entered their room on her heels, closing the door quietly behind her. She wanted to fall on him, but the words moved faster.

"You should've told me. Told me she called for you. Told me you were going to her. Told me—"

"I know." He rubbed a hand down his face. "I want to say that I didn't tell you because I didn't want you to sway me, but the truth is, I didn't want you to see I was weak enough to even entertain her."

Lithia studied him, then looked past him. "I don't know if I'm enough to stop her, but I know that fixing Suviel will be her downfall." Her voice lowered. "But you can't hesitate again."

Cal stepped into her, pulling her close. "Never."

She met him halfway, digging her fingertips into the muscle at his hips before curling them around his belt and pulling his hips in to meet hers. He unbuckled her belts, sending them clanking to the floor, pushing her back toward the wide bed, never removing his mouth from hers.

It was breathtaking the way they both fell into each other. A buzzing tingle erupted across Lia's skin as his fingertips tracked their way up the planes of her stomach toward her breasts. Calcas devoured her like he was born knowing the exact curve of her mouth, and he swallowed her moan as he rolled one of her nipples between his fingers.

He moved slowly, placing white hot kisses down her throat, and she arched into his mouth as he shifted her shirt to the side and nipped at her collarbone.

She groaned, "off."

Cal chuckled and continued his trail, pressing his weight further into her as she pushed lightly at his shoulders.

"Take it off." Her attempt at a growl was more a grunt of frustration.

Cal relented, moving to the side to pull her dirtied leathers off her body, immediately resuming his trail of open-mouthed kisses on the newly exposed skin, after tossing them to the floor.

"Yours...too," she insisted as he took a nipple into his mouth.

Cal leaned up, nipping at her ear before he spoke, "Stop giving me commands, little dragon, and let me have my way with you."

She whimpered quietly and arched her back, pressing her chest to his, the fabric of his shirt scraping her sensitive nipples. Calcas captured her mouth as he splayed a hand on her thigh, dimpling the flesh there as his fingers dug in.

He moved quickly, using her thigh to flip her onto her knees and pushing her knees apart and groaning as she pressed her chest into the bed. There was a breath before his mouth was on her, diving into her, hot tongue swirling around her clit, pulling whimpering moans from her as she ground into him.

He slid two fingers into her, whispering praises as her body began to tremble slightly. She felt the velvet soft touch of his shadows as they curled up around her legs, whispering over her oversensitive skin. He removed his fingers, shifting with a thud as his belt hit the wood of the floor.

Lithia let out another whimper, and the smooth shadows slipped further up her body, wrapping around her throat softly, caressing. There was a rush of lightning up her spine as the head of his cock brushed her entrance. He sank into her with one stroke, at the same moment tightening the shadows around her throat forcing her deep breaths into small pants. Her body lit as she moaned, deep in her throat.

"Fuck you feel—" Cal's head landed on her shoulder as he groaned.

Then he moved. He thrust deeply, wrapping the long end of her braid around his wrist, pulling lightly. The sensation was so much, too much.

"Goddess—Cal— I'm—please—"

Cal deepened his forceful strokes, muttering a string of unintelligible words as his grip on her hip tightened.

"Touch—"

He slid his hand around, finding her clit and beginning a pattern of steady circles timed with his thrusts. It made Lithia's body begin to tremble as the pleasure built at the base of her spine. Cal's shadows coiled around her wrists, bringing them together above her head, arching her back further into the soft mattress as he leaned into her ear.

"You can't possibly know how beautiful it is to watch you fall apart on my cock."

She moaned, and the shadows around her throat tightened again as the pleasure exploded behind her eyes.

"FUCK, Lia."

Cal roared as she convulsed around him, his strokes became erratic before he stilled with a throaty groan, his shadows tightened once more before they released entirely and slid down her body like water.

He slid out of her and rolled her to her back, kissing her deeply.

"I love you, little dragon."

He kissed her again before lifting her into his arms and carrying her to the bathing room and summoning the stream of hot water from the holes in the ceiling. He stood Lia in the spray and gently began washing her body. She closed her eyes, allowing his hands to explore every inch of her skin. To pull through the knots in her hair and massage her scalp. To dry her with a soft cloth before lifting her and placing her back in the bed and curling around her as she drifted off.

CALCAS

A few hours beyond sunset, they gathered in the small study attached to Neda's rooms. The castle's quiet watchfulness remained, but now it hummed with an undercurrent of expectation. A map of Suviel lay stretched across the central table. Three stones lay on the map in the places where they collected the first three shards of Suviel's magic. Two more stones lay to the side, awaiting their place.

Tadhg stood near the fire, talking quietly as he healed the cut on Neda's thigh.

"Seren sounds like she's not going to wait anymore," he said, voice edged with a weariness Cal had never heard from him. "She wanted you to have a choice before. To choose her. Now that you haven't—"

Neda added, "We need to move before she finds a way to shatter the veil before we can get to all the pieces."

Lia leaned forward in her seat. "Dragos is next. If we believe it to be on Darke Mountain, then we'll need to go there first."

"The archives there should have detailed information about the mountain as well as its inhabitants, so we can narrow down the search area. The mountain is dangerous, and I want to say as few of us as possible should go." Cal sighed. "But after this morning, I think we should be ready for Seren at any moment."

"Isn't Darke Mountain cursed?" Tadhg asked quietly.

Wil snorted. "Everything's cursed lately."

Tadhg's expression grew sober. "The volcano, it's been silent for centuries. If Seren breaks that seal before we get to it..."

"She won't," Lithia said, her voice sharp. "We'll leave in the morning."

Cal rested his hand on the hilt of his weapon. "Dragos will be under the control of my mother's advisors in her absence. Wil, can you let them know we are coming?" She nodded. "Neda, can you and Nylian get supplies tonight?"

Neda nodded as she moved toward the doors with long strides. Wil quietly followed on her heels.

Lia's voice was soft. "Get some sleep, Tadhg, you healed many today and you need to rest."

Tadhg smiled, reaching out to squeeze Lia's hand before disappearing as well.

"That went quicker than expected," she said as they started down the hall toward their own room.

"I think the end is coming into view. That always narrows the plan. There isn't much we know other than the mountain for now anyway," he said, locking the door behind him.

The fire in their room crackled low as Cal sat on the edge of the bed, undressing for bed. Lithia leaned against the doorframe, arms crossed, watching him with a careful gaze.

He finished folding his leggings and placing them on his boots, and looked up into her eyes.

"Are you afraid?"

She didn't flinch.

"Yes. It would be foolish not to be."

He held her gaze, leaning in. "Then I'll fight every inch of that with you. If it takes my life or what's left of my soul, I'll stand in her way. I swear it."

Fernholme's light was softer in the morning, a pale, sleepy hue that bled through the trees in loose threads of gold. The short battle had left its mark. Fallen branches, scorched roots, and faint trails of blood still lined the edge of the grove, but the Tree of Beginnings pulsed faintly in the center, unbroken.

Cal stood at the outer railing of the castle's garden hall, arms folded, the cool morning wind pulling hair from his topknot. Below, the canopy shimmered with dew, the sounds of life waking up filling the calm—distant voices, the soft snap of someone tightening a strap, the slide of steel being oiled, the tink of a farrier's hammer.

Around him, the others began to gather.

Wil arrived first, carrying a tray of tea and bread, correctly assuming he had passed by his own breakfast spread. She set it on the bench beside him without a word, then joined him in leaning against the railing.

"Two hours," she said quietly.

"For what?"

"For Neda to threaten to murder Tadhg," Wil smiled as the bright off-key tune of someone whistling floated down the hall.

Cal huffed a dry laugh. "One."

The tension from the previous morning clung to the air. It hadn't fully cleared, and it wouldn't until the grove and the rest of Suviel were reordered. Seren. The shards. The voiding magic that was slowly tearing apart the world, piece by piece. Cal didn't think he'd ever fully shake the feeling of dread, the weight of it crawling beneath his skin like shadows that stretched too far. And

Lithia…His gaze flicked toward the castle's entrance, expecting her to arrive any moment.

The faint sound of a floor creaking broke into his thoughts. His muscles relaxed instinctively. He didn't have to turn to know who it was. He felt the shift in the air before she spoke.

"Are we ready?" she asked, her voice stronger than the night before.

Cal glanced over his shoulder and offered a half smile, though it didn't quite reach his eyes. "As ready as we'll ever be."

Lithia stepped beside him, her expression unreadable as she stared out at the morning. The weight of what they were facing seemed to settle heavily between all of them. The past few days had been a blur of decisions made, battles fought, and promises whispered in the dark. She stood in front of them seemingly unchanged by the chaos that had surrounded them, but Cal could see the strain in the way she held herself. It was different now. She was different.

"You're quiet," Cal noted, his voice edged in concern.

Lithia's gaze flicked to him, softening so he could see the weariness in her eyes. "I'm just thinking," she replied simply, pulling her braid over her shoulder, smoothing out the messy strands as if the motion could pull her thoughts together.

He nodded, taking her hand.

Lithia turned her head slightly, looking back out over the grove. The trees were stretching in the soft light, but it felt like the calm before the storm. Too many questions, too few answers. The world was unravelling at the seams, and they were barely holding it together.

"We'll need to be prepared for The Hunt to show up at any moment," Lithia said to the group. "We can't afford to be caught off guard again."

Cal glanced at her, his gaze full of purpose. "Agreed," he replied. "We know what to expect, but we also know that Seren's more unpredictable than any of us anticipated, and the mountain's still a mystery. We don't even know where exactly it's hiding the shard."

"Alright then. Ready to move? We should make it to Dragos by tomorrow night, we can camp in the Dying Wood tonight."

LITHIA

Lithia breathed it in deeply, as if she could inhale anything that felt familiar in a world that seemed to tilt ever more sideways as time passed. The path ahead twisted through the edge of the Oak Wilds, dense mist rolling like a quiet tide along the forest floor. It was a sanctuary of wild and raw magic. The air was thick with the kind of magic that clung to the ancient trees like an old secret, slipping between the roots and the branches. Every step deeper into the mist made her nerves pull taut, each breath thicker than the last. She patted Daylis's neck in comfort as they moved.

Cal and Redmaw walked beside them, not quite close enough to touch, but close enough that she could feel his presence like the crackling warmth of a fire. His shadows always near, coiled and uncoiled around them both.

The Oak Wilds were only the first of many barriers they had to cross to reach Dargos. She glanced at Cal out of the corner of her eye. His gaze was focused ahead, his expression calmly blank, and she wondered if he was discomforted by the feel of magic or if it was just the weight of their journey.

"How much farther?" Neda asked behind them, voice heavy with exhaustion. Lithia had lost track of time somewhere between now and when they left the city gates, the endless repetitiveness of the woods lulling her. The air felt strained, every shadow longer than it should be, as if the land itself was holding its breath.

"Not far," Lithia answered, her voice thick. She cleared her throat, forcing her mind to the task at hand.

The Oak Wilds had their own rhythm, and Lithia could feel it thrum around them. Every step took them deeper into the fold of its silence as the fog curled tighter and the trees narrowed. A foghorn in the distance reminded her of the sea, mournful and endless, but the thought was fleeting.

As if on cue, the fog parted ahead, revealing a path lined with gnarled, twisted trees, their bark dark and scorched as though something had burned through them long ago and never truly left. The Dying Wood. It was said to be where the boundary between the living and the dead blurred, but in reality, it was just the transition from fog thick forest to scorched desert.

Lithia pulled Daylis to a stop just inside the Wilds. "We can make camp, but we'll leave at dawn. No delays." She could already feel the unease creeping in, the chill of the place tugging at her limbs. She needed to move, to do something, anything, to keep her mind from wandering.

The fire was set quickly as Neda and Wil worked in silence, but Lithia couldn't seem to find peace in the flickering light. Her hands were too restless, her thoughts too loud. The weight of the magic that had taken residence in her chest groaned.

"I've never liked coming here," Cal's voice broke the quiet, startling her. He moved to sit beside her, his eyes glinting in the dimming light. She met his gaze for the first time all day, and something in the weight of his stare made her breath catch.

"The Wilds feel overwhelming."

Lithia hesitated, then pulled her knees to her chest, wrapping her arms around them. Her eyes swept over the group, watching as Wil and Neda conversed in hushed tones, the campfire flickering between them.

He reached out, his hand hovering above hers before he gently grasped it, his fingers warm against the chill of the air. His thumb brushed lightly over her knuckles, the silence between them stretching into something comfortable. She turned her gaze to his hand holding hers, the quiet strength in him grounding her when everything else seemed on the edge of splintering.

The night deepened around them, the chill of the Oak Wilds creeping into her bones. She shivered and moved into Calcas as the firelight danced across the faces of the others. They didn't speak again until the stars began to bleed through the thinning clouds above them.

Lithia coughed as sand scratched at her lungs as they made their way through the twisting paths of scorched trees, their bark dark and slick with some unnatural rot. The Dying Wood was a thin stretch of forest, so they wouldn't have to contend with the smell of decay for long, but it was vile.

Cal, silent beside her, kept his hand near his weapon, his shadow wrapping around them both like an unseen barrier. He was watching the trees carefully. Lithia could feel the weight of his attention, but she couldn't afford to be distracted.

At midday, they stopped at a small clearing to rest. The sun was high, the heat growing heavier as they moved, the trees becoming sparser around them.

"We're close," Lithia murmured, swallowing mouthfuls of water before passing the skin to Cal. "It's not far now."

The final leg of the journey was short, the stretch of desert between the Dying Wood and the city gate at Dragos only taking them a couple of hours to reach. They passed under the large stone arch into the city at the hottest part of the day and made their way through the outer rings of the city in silence as it bustled with people.

The nearer the city's center they came, the more the crowd thinned, the people moving slower and less deliberately. After nearly an hour, they found themselves in the prime's manor in the city center. It was a palatial, but unlike the other courts, it was separate from the working buildings used by the arcane leadership, so when they entered, it was quiet with just the few staff milling about to greet them.

Lithia had always loved visiting Cal here. It felt so different from the state buildings that had dominated the majority of their childhood. It was just...a home. A tall fae in formal robes stepped out of the sitting room to the right with a warm smile on his face.

"Welcome home, nephew."

"Bracken," Cal said. He smiled broadly and moved to embrace his uncle.

They hugged and spoke quietly as they moved further into the house. The rest of the party followed, and Lithia smiled quietly to herself as she watched Cal, so genuinely happy to see his uncle.

They walked down the polished black marble hall toward the dining room, where they all gratefully fell into open seats. They ate quietly as Cal filled his uncle in on what they were doing.

"I've already alerted the archives that you will be coming in the morning. I'll send them a note tonight and have some of their acolytes pull what you need so it's waiting for you." Bracken's voice was low and smooth like Calcas, and they had the same playful smirk when they smiled.

"Thank you, that will help. Could you also find me a few amphiptere riders who would be willing to come talk to us?"

Calcas

Above the prime's offices and meeting hall, in the labyrinthine corridors of Dragos's ancient archives, Cal, Lithia, and the rest of the group sifted through scrolls, manuscripts, and maps. The vastness of the archives felt oppressive, the endless shelves full of knowledge pressing in from all sides.

Cal leaned over a large, weathered map spread across the stone table. His fingers traced the lines of Darke Mountain, eyes narrowing as he studied the jagged peaks. Beside him, Lithia traced her own path on the map, her brow furrowed in concentration.

"I've been through this stack a hundred times," Neda muttered, half under her breath, as she sorted through a pile of old manuscripts. "But there's just nothing there. The mountain, the shard...are we sure it's there?"

Cal ran a hand through his hair. His frustration was evident in the set of his jaw. "We need answers quickly, and it seems like the most logical place for it to be based on where we've found the others. There's a concentration of magic there. It's a natural center of the court. It's protected by the land. It makes sense."

"I found something," Tadhg hopped up, holding up a tattered scroll. "The amphipteres hoard anything of value, and they're drawn to powerful magic. If we get too close to their nests, they'll know we're there, we know all of that, *but*, this says they only lay their eggs in one area, moving the young to their nests once they hatch. It's fiercely guarded, it's high on the mountain. That has to be it."

Lithia tilted her head, her eyes sharp. "Bracken sent word that the amphiptere riders are more than happy to talk with us. They may know more, having interacted with some of the nesting females."

The sun was high and blazed down on the cobbled streets. They were mounted and ready, supplies packed as they made their way to the eastern edge of the city, toward the rookery.

The riders had long been the stewards of Darke Mountain. They were known for their skill with the massive, winged serpents. If anyone could help them reach the shard safely, it was them. As a youngling, Cal had wanted to become a rider so badly, only to find he did not have the temperament required to...not die.

At the rookery's entrance, a tall woman with short-cropped black hair and dark leathers stood watching them. Her eyes were cold, but her gaze spoke of hard-won experience.

"Bracken said you've come to ask about the mountain," she said, her voice low and even. Her gaze flicked to each of them in turn. "I'm Tempris."

Cal replied, his voice steady. "We need to know about the amphipteres, their nesting and laying grounds, and the way through them."

Tempris's lips twisted. "You're not the first to think they can get past the amphipteres. The nests are sacred to them. They don't take kindly to intruders."

Neda stepped forward. "We're not here to provoke them. We just need the way in and out. And if you can help us avoid the dangers—"

Tempris's expression softened just a fraction, but only for a moment. "In and out." She let out a quiet, almost imperceptible laugh, crossing her arms across her chest. "There's no 'in and out' with the amphipteres. Their nesting caves are labyrinths. And if you get near one, they'll know. Their magic is drawn to power. Especially as much as you have." She gestured to Lia.

"Can you tell us about their laying cave?" Tempris's eyes flashed. "We know they lay somewhere different from where they nest, we think what we are searching for is there, it's why they are drawn there."

"We don't have a choice," Cal followed.

Tempris softened as her eyes scanned them.

She sighed, then motioned into the rookery. "I'll show you to my mount, Citha. She's the only one who might get you near the nests without being killed. But understand this, if we take her into that mountain and something goes wrong, you're on your own."

The rider led them through the rookery to a large cave, where an amphiptere lay curled. Its scales were a dark, iridescent black, its long body coiled with a fluid grace that belied its size. Citha was beautiful in a terrifying way that starkly contrasted Othis, her body exuding raw power.

"This is Citha," Tempris said, brushing a hand over the creature's side. The amphiptere's eyes flicked toward her, a deep rumble emanating from its throat as it acknowledged her presence. "She's bonded to me and knows the mountain better than anyone, and she is a nesting female. Her clutch hatched a few weeks ago, but even she can't guarantee your safety if you venture into their territory and anger another nesting female."

Tadhg stared at Citha, his expression one of awe. "She's beautiful."

Temptis smiled, and Citha made the deep rumbling noise in the back of her throat again. "Everything about the mountain is dangerous. Simple as that."

Lithia bowed her head to Citha. "We know, we wouldn't be here if we had any other choice."

Tempris nodded, her face hardening once again.

As they prepared to leave, Tempris mounted Citha with a fluid motion, becoming one with the creature's sleek body. Cal and the others mounted their horses before they followed in the shadow of Tempris and Citha as they flew toward Darke Mountain. The mountain loomed ahead, dark and brooding, smoke rolling from its top, clogging the sky as it grew larger with each step.

LITHIA

The wind was hot and harsh, carrying with it the acrid scent of sulfur from the volcano at the mountain's summit. Below them, the land stretched out dark and jagged like the spine of some forgotten creature. The earth itself, carved in the image of something monstrous.

Citha, moved with a quiet grace above them, her dark wings cutting through the air in slow, deliberate beats that stirred the grit under her feet. Tempris kept a tight hold on her mount, her posture confident as ever, her eyes constantly scanning ahead.

They approached a narrow gorge, and the path wound through sharp rocks that seemed to close in on them from all sides. Lia's body was tight with tension as the nesting mothers shifted to peer down at them as they passed.

Tempris landed Citha at the end of the narrowing gorge, signaling for them to stop. Ahead, the path opened to a bowl just before the face of the mountain rose dramatically like a wall, a large gash the only indication that there was any where forward to continue.

She turned in the saddle to face them, her voice low. "This is where we part ways," she said. "This is the entrance to the laying grounds. We won't follow you in. You'll need to navigate it your-selves. You won't be able to continue on horseback, but they will be safe tied in the gorge. Be safe...and quiet."

Neda's brows furrowed. "Navigate it?" She glanced around, uncertainty flickering across her face.

Tempris didn't answer right away. Her gaze flicked over them, taking in their apprehension before speaking again.

"The amphipteres are the guardians of this mountain. They don't just protect their nests. As I said at the rookery, their nesting caves are labyrinths...I would expect the caves you are about to enter to be much the same. A shifting maze of stone and magic. Nothing stays in place for long. If you stray off course...You may never find your way back, but if you are successful, they are likely to protect you since the mountain granted you passage."

There was a pause. No one spoke. The air felt heavier, as though the mountain itself held its breath with them.

"Isn't there anything we can do to avoid angering them?" Tadhg asked, his voice calmer than Lithia expected. "The amphiptere I've interacted with have never been nesting or laying."

Tempris let out a short laugh. "You can try, but the amphipteres are drawn to magic. The moment you step foot in there, they'll know. Be quiet, move slowly, touch nothing. Many of the ones in the laying caves will be males. We don't interact with males often, so I can't help much with their temperament, but they will be protective of any egg and female present."

"We'll make it work," Lithia said, her voice stronger than she felt. "We don't have a choice."

Tempris nodded slowly, her expression bored. "Good luck," she said flatly. "Don't expect any help if things go wrong."

Lia saw Cal's fingers twitch at his side, instinctively moving toward the hilt of his blade. The mountain was suffocating, each breath heavy with the knowledge of how little they knew about what they were walking into. But they had no choice. Seren wouldn't wait for them to prepare, so they had to move.

With that, she urged Citha upward, her wings lifting them both into the air. They vanished into the swirling clouds, their forms barely visible against the backdrop of the mountains.

"I hate this place already," Neda muttered, her horse shifting nervously as she dismounted.

Tadhg snorted. "Oh, it's only going to get worse, we should have called Othis."

Wil tilted her head, staring into the mountain. "He would not have come."

They all turned to her to find that a small smile was tugging the corner of her mouth.

"Othis is dead, Tadhg. He can not return to this place. He could only come to us in the valley because the veil is fading. He is usually bound to the same places as my father. The Beneath, the temple, and the Pass of Souls."

Tadhg stared slack-jawed at Wil, who had begun to laugh quietly at his shock.

"I never—I didn't ever consider that."

"Come on, we can do this without him. He would be a pest anyway."

They moved forward, footsteps slow and deliberate. The walls of the gorge widened with each step, and the ground grew uneven. Each breath was thick with ash and magic, suffocating her. The mountain watched, waiting for them to falter.

"I don't trust this," Neda muttered again. "This whole mountain feels...wrong."

"Feelings are only going to slow us down," Lithia said, her voice tight. She pulled her braid over her shoulder, fingers tugging at the strands absentmindedly. "Focus."

Lithia felt a tingle of magic dance over her skin as they entered the mountain. They came to a vast and hollow cavern that stretched beyond their sight. The walls were smooth as though polished by an unseen hand, and the stone gleamed in the flickering of several pit fires.

"There's something wrong," Lithia murmured, her voice barely a whisper as she reached out to touch the wall.

The stone shuddered beneath her fingers, a faint pulse reverberating through the air.

"There's magic," Neda said softly, stepping closer beside her. "I can feel it. It's singing?"

"Don't touch it," Tadhg warned, his voice harsh. "Tempris just warned us—"

He was cut off by a low rumble that echoed through the chamber, making Lithia's teeth rattle. The ground beneath them shook, and the walls started to shift, closing in on them with a slow, grinding groan.

Cal grabbed Lithia, pulling her away from the wall just as the stone beneath them cracked open, splitting apart in irregular gashes.

But Lithia had already pulled her hand back, her brow furrowed in concentration. "This is a part of the labyrinth."

"Move!" Cal shouted, his voice urgent.

They barely had time to react as the ground split further, and the open cavern became a narrow passageway, swallowed by the mountain's shifting walls.

"So much for slow," Cal said, his voice taut. "Move, now!"

They scrambled forward, urgency pushing them deeper into the labyrinth. The walls around them groaned and shifted, each step deeper into the mountain seeming to twist their path. The air was hot, each breath a struggle.

And then, as though it had been waiting for her, the path opened into another chamber. This one was different. It was wider, its walls jagged and torn, as though something had clawed its way through the stone. At the center of the room was a wraith wrapped in The Hunt's gleaming armor.

Calcas

The chamber hummed with tension. The labyrinth had opened up directly into a trap. The walls caged them in with a predator. The wraith stood, its opaline armor shining in the low firelight. He had known this moment was imminent, but no one could have prepared for the brutal reality of being caught like a mouse in a trap.

Cal's heart beat in time with the pulsing walls. The wraith stood motionless in the center of the chamber, its head encased in a helmet with no eyes, no mouth, just smooth, featureless metal. The chamber began to fill with a thick, viscous fog.

A ripple of movement behind the wraith caused Cal's hand to tighten on the hilt of his morningstar. Another figure emerged, a tall, wiry fae with a wild mane of dark hair, his form similarly wrapped in The Hunt's armor. His gaze was cold, the cruel smile on his lips sharp enough to split stone. He carried a spear, long and wicked, its head glowing faintly.

The man with the spear grinned, his blackened teeth gleaming beneath his helm. "Did you think you could sneak past us?" His voice was full of malice. "The labyrinth hides many things, doesn't it?"

Cal's muscles ripped as he slid the weapon from his back. "We have bigger problems to solve than the two of you," he said, his voice low and steady.

He saw Neda from the corner of his eye as she pulled her bow from her back, nocking an arrow. "Don't have to sneak if you're dead," she muttered under her breath.

The wraith did not respond, its form flickering and shifting like smoke in the wind. It seemed to bend the air around it, distorting the space. The labyrinth had a life of its own, and it was no friend to any intruder.

The wraith's hand twitched, his spear flashing forward in a blur of motion. Cal barely managed to block it with his morningstar, the impact sending a jolt up his arm. The spearhead slid along the shaft with a sound like tearing metal. A taunting laugh bounced off the walls as he swung again, the spear a blur of lethal precision.

He moved, putting all his force into his swing, his morningstar coming down in a swift arc to deflect the blow. The two of them were locked in a dance of steel, each strike and counterstrike echoing through the chamber, their movements a blur of controlled violence.

Wil was the next to move. Silently, she closed the distance between herself and the faceless wraith, her short sword a blur of silver. She slashed at the wraith's armor, but it shifted with inhuman speed, its body flickering like a mirage, the blade passing harmlessly through its smoky form.

The wraith's voice echoed through the chamber, as disembodied and hollow as the mountain itself. "You are not worthy," it hissed, its words a low, vibrating pulse in the air. "None of you are."

Lithia lunged toward the wraith, daggers gleaming in her hands. She twisted around the wraith's flailing form, aiming for any gap in its shimmering armor. But the wraith was like liquid, constantly shifting, reforming, its form never quite solid enough to be pinned down. Lithia's daggers found nothing but empty air.

"Damned ghost," she muttered under her breath, frustration seeping through her tone.

Cal had barely managed to recover from the wraith's last blow when the chamber turned against them. A deafening crack echoed through the room, and the ground beneath them split open, sending stones tumbling in every direction. The labyrinth was shifting once more. The walls moved, closing in with brutal force, trying to swallow them whole.

"Move!" Wil shouted.

The walls began to constrict, the floor warping and buckling like claws digging into the center of the chamber. A terrible screech filled the air, reverberating off the walls as the amphiptere swooped down into the chamber, its massive wings beating the air in a thunderous rhythm. Its gleaming scales shone like fire, and its glowing eyes locked onto them each in turn.

The amphiptere let out a low hiss, its fangs bared as it undulated its long, serpentine body on the ground before them.

A male. Cal scanned the newly formed hall, finding both wraiths had vanished into the labyrinth, and instead, they stood in a narrow hall with several carved alcoves. His eyes caught the problem immediately. The nearest alcove to them held a sleeping female amphiptere curled around a clutch of glittering red and purple eggs. The alcove down on the left looked to be the start of another passageway, which was likely to be their best option.

He saw the others slowly and silently catch sight of the danger and scanned, looking for their next movement. They could wait and hope the mountain shifted quickly, but they needed to move forward, and he was sure that staying still would drop them somewhere just as bad.

The male amphiptere watched them, eyes narrowed, but didn't make any moves to attack. Tempris said to be quiet, move slowly, and not touch anything, so he whispered.

"We need to very slowly sheath our weapons to clear our hands so it can tell we aren't here to take its eggs, then we should start backing very slowly toward the alcove to the left, which looks like the next passage."

He got several nearly imperceptible nods as he so slowly slid his morningstar into one of the loops on his belt rather than attempting to lift it over his head into its holster. It would be awkward to walk with for a bit, but he could deal with it later.

Cal slowly began moving toward the wall to his left, keeping his body facing the protective serpent in front of him. They moved excruciatingly slowly as it tracked every step. Just before they reached the passage entrance, someone tripped on the uneven ground, causing an ear-splitting screech from the amphiptere. Cal looked sharply toward the sound of the noise and found Lia, rather than facing the beast or cowering, was...bowing.

The screeching stopped as it took in Lia's position. After several seconds, it lowered into a bow of its own, bringing its head level with them. It huffed a stream of hot air at them, and they continued, backing into the passage. Cal didn't breathe again until the creature and its nesting female were out of sight.

The new passage was pitch dark and winding. Cal conjured a small flame to light their path as they moved slowly through the mountain once more. As they came through a sharp curve, the tunnel opened abruptly, the ceiling falling away far above them and the walls grinding as they slid apart.

Cal's flame went out, plunging them into darkness, and they were left without light as the mountain around them shifted. After several minutes of the deafening sound of rock on rock, light flooded Cal's eyes. He blinked hard as his eyes adjusted, taking in the room before them.

A pillar of flaming magic rose from the center of the room, veins of shadow swirling through it in an endless spiral.

"We made it?"

Lithia's voice sounded fragile. She took a single step forward as a great black shadow dropped from the ceiling, landing with a thunderous crash on the far side of the shard.

"Seren," Cal breathed, his stomach sinking.

LITHIA

Lithia's body seized as she watched Seren slip from the amphiptere's back. Seren's long brown hair whipped around her face, and the cloak that hung from her shoulders was dark, blending seamlessly into the shadows. Her golden eyes were sharp and unforgiving, and there was no softness left in the way she regarded them.

"Seren, please," Cal said, his voice strained.

Her lips curled into a thin smile. "I know what's at stake, Cal. *You* know what's at stake. But this is not your fight to win." Her hand went to the hilt of her blade, and the amphiptere's wings stirred restlessly behind her, a sign of the danger to come.

The amphiptere behind Seren stirred, its enormous form rippling as it flexed its wings, its body a perfect embodiment of predatory power.

Lithia's breath slowed as she watched the gleam of Seren's blade. She could see it now, the sharp curve of the hilt, the way Seren's fingers curled around it. Lithia slid her hand toward the sword of Mab, letting its warmth creep up her arm, waiting for the inevitable clash.

"It doesn't have to be like this," Cal said, his voice urgent. "Seren, I—"

"No," Seren cut him off. "It *must* be like this. You've failed me for the last time, Calcas. I gave you, all of you, a chance, but you chose your side, and now you'll suffer the consequences of that choice."

Cal's eyes flickered toward Lithia, his expression briefly softening before solidifying again, a silent apology mixed with resolve. She could see he was trying to find a way to reach her, to desperately grasp at the fragments of the person he once loved, but Seren...Seren was lost to them once more.

Lithia's pulse quickened as she watched her lover become the distant shadow of what she had been in life as death rotted her soul. This was no longer the Seren she had known. This was a force of destruction, an unstoppable tide of fury wrapped in beauty.

"I'm not here to fight you, Seren," Lithia spoke, her voice steady despite the turmoil churning in her chest. "But if it comes to that, we will stop you. I won't let you destroy the world."

Seren laughed. It was more cruel than anything Lithia had heard fall from her lips. It echoed off the walls, mocking her.

"Stop me? You think you can stop me, Lia?" she asked, her voice dripping with condescension. "You always wanted to fix things without touching them, with hollow gestures of peace and hasty promises. But you've never understood the true cost of power. You still don't."

Lithia's fingers flexed around her hilt. "I've learned a lot since the moment I shattered as the life left your body."

Seren flinched.

The amphiptere's wings moved forward, opening with a deafening *whoosh*, and the air shifted again. Seren stepped forward out of the curl of her mount.

"You can't win this fight, Lia," Seren murmured, "You're out of your depth."

"Maybe," Lithia replied, her voice steadier. "But it was you who pushed me into the waves."

Seren's mask faltered for a moment, a flicker of emotion crossing her face. It was gone in an instant, replaced by a cold, predatory stare as she summoned her crowned helm, and her eyes disappeared from view.

The silence between them stretched thin, like the calm before a storm. Then, with a suddenness that shattered the tension, Seren lunged forward, the amphiptere's wings flapping behind her in a chaotic gust of wind.

Lithia barely had time to react. Her own darkened blade shimmered with veins of magic as she pushed it through the blade.

She met Seren's strike with a clash that sent a shockwave of energy through the air, reverberating in her chest, stealing her breath.

Blades grinding, sparks splashed like colliding stars as Lithia blocked Seren's onslaught. Seren's every move was a storm, wild and untamable, intent on crushing anyone in her path.

Lithia's feet skidded in the dirt as she fought for ground, twisting her body to deflect a downward strike that could have cleaved her in two. The air around them hummed, the amphiptere's wings beating in rhythmic synchronization with Seren's movements.

Seren spun, her blade cutting a wide arc that Lithia barely managed to avoid, the steel grazing the side of her armor. Lithia's heart pounded in her chest, her pulse erratic as she regained her footing. She tightened her grip on Mab's hilt, summoning any shard of magic and letting it surge through her limbs. The sword hummed in response, a deep, ancient resonance that was both familiar and grounding.

The air between them crackled, and Lithia launched herself at Seren, her sword raised high. She brought it down in a swift, fluid motion, but Seren was already gone, a blur in the shadows. Lithia's strike cut through the air, missing its target by mere inches.

Seren's laugh set Lithia's teeth on edge. As she reappeared behind her, blade already slashing toward Lithia's side. The strike was vicious, and Lithia barely managed to twist away, feeling the breath leave her lungs as she staggered. Her heart raced as she turned to face her again, but Seren was relentless, pressing her attacks, each one faster than the last.

Lithia's mind raced, calculating her options. She couldn't keep up with Seren's speed—not in raw strength, or fury. She needed to outthink her, outmaneuver her.

With a flick of her sword, Lithia launched a surge of magic from her blade directly at Seren's chest. It was a gamble, but Seren barely had time to react, caught off guard as the dark pulse hit her squarely, sending her crashing back against the amphiptere's massive frame.

The amphiptere shrieked, its wings flaring, causing a gust of wind that sent debris flying. Seren staggered to her feet, slinging her helm from her head, revealing a face twisted in rage.

"You think that's enough to stop me?" Seren hissed, blood dripping from her lip as her gaze darkened.

"No," Lithia said, her voice low.

Lithia lunged forward, eyes narrowed, determination coursing through her veins.

With a roar, Seren twisted away, her blade slicing the air in a deadly arc aimed at Lithia's throat. The deadly strike came too fast, too close, until, at the last moment, a figure stepped in front of Lithia, blocking the blow with a solid clang of steel.

"Enough." Cal's voice was like a final desperate prayer.

There was a heartbeat, a moment of pure stillness as all three stood on the precipice of fate.

Seren's eyes flashed, burning with fury, but the moment of hesitation gave Lithia the chance she needed to see her opening. With a devastating cry, Seren swung her blade at Cal, her fury unleashing in a wave of dark energy. Lithia saw it in that instant, the terrible beauty of Seren's power, but also the loss.

LITHIA

She didn't hesitate.

Lithia's heart hammered in her chest as she felt the sudden shift of power in the air. The world around her seemed to shrink, collapsing into a singular point of focus—the shard. The swirling mass of flame and shadow pulsated in the center of the room, and the magic it emanated called to her like a siren's song.

Without sparing another glance for Seren, she sprinted forward, rushing toward the pillar of fire. She had to reach this shard. And she had to reach the next. She had to stop this void before it consumed everything.

The moment her fingers brushed the surface of the shard, molten heat tore through her body. Her skin screamed in protest, and she could feel the shard's magic coiling around her core like chains, tightening with every breath she took. The shard's magic latched onto her with the force of a tempest threatening to rip her apart.

"Lia!" Cal's voice cracked through the noise, thick with fear.

Lithia tried to yank her hand back, but it was too late. She was already too far in. The magic from the shard burned through her like wildfire, searing her veins, consuming her thoughts. She could feel it twisting and contorting inside her, and she fought to breathe as the heat dug its claws into her core.

Her vision faltered, darkening at the edges. Her knees buckled, the world spinning as she struggled to stay upright, to keep control, but the energy swelled around her with a force that she wasn't sure she could withstand.

"Please…" She could barely breathe the word, her voice barely a whisper in the roaring maelstrom.

She watched frozen in place as the chamber continued its descent into chaos, Neda and Tadgh moving behind her as Wil moved to help Calcas push Seren back. Wil took a vicious swing at the amphiptere as it attempted to throw her from Ser with its tail. She took a breath to warn Wil as the creature reared back to strike at her, when fire flooded her veins once more, and she screamed.

The pain was overwhelming. Her limbs grew heavy, like lead, while her body screamed for release from the suffocating magic. She couldn't escape it. She could *feel* it settling into her bones, taking up all available space. Where the earth magic had slipped into her, comforting and grounding, the arcane magic needed Lia to feel the destruction it was capable of.

"Lia." Cal's voice reached her again, a whisper of terror that she could barely make out through the chaos in her head. His footsteps faltered beside her, but she couldn't focus, couldn't move. Her soul was being ripped in half.

The shard's magic wove its tendrils deeper, threading through her mind, her body, her very essence. *It's too much,* she thought. *I can't handle it. I can't—*

Her vision went black. She felt each part of her body burn to ash, only to be reformed and burn again. She was a phoenix stuck in the cycle of death and rebirth, feeling the pain of each death in an endless loop of agony.

A single breath broke through the fog of magic, one quiet word.

"Lia?" Cal's voice again, but this time it was closer, more frantic. "Little Dra–"

His voice cut off suddenly, and a new one filled her mind.

"I'm sorry, Lia."

The words were soft, a whispered apology that she hadn't heard in far too long. Lithia's heart stilled, a chill running down her spine as her mind slowly clawed its way back into consciousness.

It was Seren.

Lithia's eyes snapped open, her surroundings spinning, the world shifting before her. The world pulsed around her, disorienting, and in that confusion, there was a flash of clear movement.

Seren.

Her golden eyes were unforgiving as she appeared from the shadows, a twisted version of the woman she once knew. The amphiptere spread its wings, and Lithia's breath caught in her throat as she saw Cal, limp and lifeless, draped across the creature's back. His blood stained the dark feathers of the beast, the sight of it sinking deep into Lithia's heart like a dagger.

"*No...*" Lithia tried to move, but the shard's magic had her rooted in place.

The panic closed in on her, tightening around her chest as the weight of the scene pressed in. She watched as the others fought against Seren's magic, reaching for Cal. But the pain in her chest wasn't just from the magic. It was the image of Cal being ripped from them that sliced into her.

And the voice of someone she once loved.

"I'm sorry, Lia."

Lithia's heart fractured as her body trembled with the fury of the magic that ravaged her, her mind going fuzzy and black as ripples of pain tore through her. She didn't have the strength to scream as Seren mounted and vanished into the light of her amphiptere's fire, Cal's limp body draped across its back.

She pushed back at the magic, but it snapped violently back like a whip, throwing her back with such force that her vision blurred. The pillar of fire was gone from her line of sight as the labyrinth shifted around her, the walls closing in tighter than ever before. She may have survived this shard, but she would not survive this loss.

One thought repeated in her mind, louder than the roaring of the magic as the world went black.

She had failed him...again.

LITHIA

The city gates had slammed closed behind them with a heavy thud that echoed in Lithia's bones. The bustling streets had been overwhelming and loud, the cobblestone s dark with the stretching shadows of the evening as the sun dipped below the walls. The air felt like it was clawing its way down her throat as they walked into the manor. Buzzing filled her ears as Wil explained to Bracken that Seren had taken Cal.

Lithia hadn't spoken since she woke on the front of Wil's horse. She hadn't spoken as she mounted Daylis or as they rode across the hot sand toward the city. She hadn't spoken to any of the fae that greeted them in the street. She hadn't even been able to look into Bracken's face because she couldn't bear to see the echo of any of Cal's features.

Tadhg had assured her countless times in the last day that Cal was very much alive when Seren left, but it didn't matter. He was gone, and it was her fault. She wasn't strong enough to take the shard and continue to fight, so she had lost him to Seren. And Seren had known exactly what loss would cause her to falter.

She had lain in the room that smelled like him and fallen asleep with the all-consuming fear that the longer he was in Seren's hands, the more chance she would never find him again. The only glimmer of hope lay in the thin thread of fate that still pulsed in her chest.

Lithia's breath formed small clouds in the night air as she quickened her pace, trying to match Bracken's long strides. Her mind raced with worry, but even more so with a growing sense of urgency.

At the front of their group, Bracken walked with a purpose. His robes billowed behind him like the dark wings of a crow. He didn't speak at first, his silence carrying further than any words could. Despite his age, there was a youthful tension in his gait, something Lithia recognized as fear. It wasn't the kind of fear that made him hesitate, but the kind that forced him to act quickly, without thought, without delay. But it was only when he stopped and turned to face them that Lithia realized just how much fear lay in his eyes.

"Tell me then, what makes you believe they would have kept him here rather than taking him to The Beneath," Bracken began, his voice weary.

Wil spoke first, "She would not risk entering The Beneath. Thahaos is watching for her and would not allow it."

Bracken nodded absently, "Do you know of anywhere they could be here in Suviel?"

Lia's shoulders curled in, her voice hoarse from disuse, "No? I don't think they would return to the mountain where we found the first shard, and I can't thin—"

Lia froze, her spine going rigid, "The voxis." She turned to the others, "The voxis in Mt. Haven, they were worried about a *she*." She turned back to Bracken, "Have you had any voxis reports recently?"

The silence that followed was heavy, pressing down on her, waiting for her to break. Lithia felt the idea sink into her, settling deeper and deeper until it lodged itself in her chest, the thread of fate thrumming in response.

"We need to find out where they are gathering," Neda's voice broke through the heavy air. "Whatever they're planning, we can't let them use him. Not as a pawn."

Bracken's eyes were glazed as he turned and started moving toward his office rather than the archives.

"There has been an alarming number of voxis actually, I've been tracking them for weeks, but they haven't done anything to warrant alarm."

He pushed through his office door, rounding his desk and frantically searching for something in the papers strewn there.

"Here," he said, pulling out a sheet, his eyes scanning, "They've been gathering in the eastern districts. That's where the armors are. But they've only been buying small, normal amounts and haven't caused any disturbances, so we've left them alone. We aren't quite sure where they are entering from, however, because there aren't many signs of them at the gates."

"Are there many?"

"Yes and no, from what we can tell, they are moving in and out of the city somehow because their numbers are fluctuating, we just haven't figured out how."

Lithia clenched her fists, trying to channel the anger that rose within her, the frustration at being unable to do anything, the helplessness that made her feel small. But there was no time for rage—not now.

"We won't go in blindly," Bracken continued. "The voxis clearly know how to move in the city expertly. We'll need to be cautious. If we rush in, we risk everything. If we lose Cal—"

Lithia sighed. "He is not in the city, Bracken."

Bracken looked up from his papers to find the four of them watching him sadly as his flash of hope fizzed out.

Wil straightened from her place by the door. "We need to find out how they are getting the weapons out of the city and where, so we can follow them. The weapons will be going wherever 'she' is. That's the best shot we have. We know the blacksmith in Mt. Haven said that's what they were looking for, so I imagine it is the same here."

Bracken spoke, his voice quiet, "I have a few contacts in the area. They know the back alleys, the hidden paths, the places where we can avoid the voxis's patrols. We should move swiftly, they could move at any moment, and we don't know how often they do."

Neda shook her head. "No, we can't risk them getting any inkling they are being followed. If they are in contact with Seren at all, I'm sure this recent development will mobilize them." She turned to Wil, her eyes softening somewhat, and Lia's throat burned at the sight. "Wil, can you send a crow instead?"

Wil nodded once. "I planned to, I think it will be best if only Lia and I go for Cal."

Neda and Tadhg both opened their mouths to respond, but were silenced by Lia's raised hand.

"I agree." Lithia's heart thundered in her chest. "We don't need to fight," she added, explaining before they could begin their arguments. "We need to find him, get him out, and leave before they know we're there."

"That may not be possible," Neda said through clenched teeth. "If Cal is being held at some sort of base they have set up, you may have to deal with more than just the voxis. They could have traps set, or any number of void poisoned creatures, or even just generally deadly creatures like the ones in the fighting pits. They'll be expecting you."

"I know, but can't waste any time or risk being caught early," Lithia said, determination flowing through her like liquid steel. "We find Cal, and we bring him back. Nothing else matters."

Tadhg cleared his throat. "Lia...should you be going at all?" Something in her expression made his face drain. "What I meant was, maybe one of us should go with Wil while you head for the final shard. We are so close, and you may be able to save all of us, *including Cal*, faster than we can."

Lithia's eyes slipped out of focus. He was right, she knew he was, but she couldn't put Cal's life on anyone else's shoulders. More than that, she wasn't sure she was strong enough to take on the last shard, and she needed her mind to be capable of focus when the time came.

She stood. "He is my mate."

The room was filled with a tense silence before Tadhg nodded once, standing beside her. She turned, leaving the room, and remained silent as they made their way back to the manor. A soft flapping of wings punctuated their movements as a crow flew east toward the glittering lights.

LITHIA

*I*t took two days.

Two days for the crow to let Wil know that the voxis were readying to move weapons through a portion of the eastern wall. There was a crack in the wall that they had glamoured to be able to come and go without having to make use of the gates. The four of them, along with two of the legion that Neda had pulled in to help, dressed and prepared to leave the city through the gates.

The plan was for Neda and Tadhg to take the two legionaries, now disguised to resemble Lithia and Willow, and head for Arachin. The hope was that the voxis would be less on alert for their presence because they had made a very public exit.

Within the hour after receiving word, the four of them exited the city gates, Wil and Lia switching places with their doubles once free of the eyes on the street. They slipped silently around the exterior wall of Dragos, until a low caw from above announced that they had found their exit.

They crouched low in the brush, Wil conjuring some form of shadow to hide them as they watched for the voxis to emerge. Several hours later, the crow cawed again, and Lithia's spine snapped straight as a small voxis seemingly stepped through the wall and into the open. They searched the area for several minutes before letting out two sharp whistles. Moments later, a larger group of voxis began pouring through the wall. Some walking and some on horseback, but none of them armed.

Lia and Wil exchanged a confused look until another whistle sounded and two horses moved through the wall pulling an overladen covered cart that clanked with each movement. Bile rose in Lia's throat as they watched the massive party pass in relative quiet. They waited for them to be entirely out of eyeline before moving out from their spot and following at a distance in silence, the crow circling far ahead.

Lithia felt every step of the road beneath her feet, a rhythm that mirrored the pounding in her head. They continued through the early evening, the air becoming cool and damp, the last vestiges of the city blotted out behind them by the time the voxis made camp. The howling wind of the dying wood greeted them first, its skeletal trees stretching like black fingers toward a bruised sky.

They could make out the group's fires through the sparse trunks of the Dying Wood as they huddled in the blackness for warmth, not willing to risk being seen for a fire.

"The crow says this is all the voxis that were in the eastern districts," Wil said quietly. "They cleared out."

A shiver ran up Lithia's spine. "Wil I—"

"Lia." Wil's voice was quiet and sure. "You're not alone in this."

Lithia nodded, her gaze locked ahead. She was right. But every breath was a reminder of her own helplessness, the constant weight of loss pressing down on her shoulders.

After another day of travel, the landscape shifted. The Dying Wood began to give way to the Oak Wilds. The air smelled of rich, damp earth, the scent of old things. It was easier to remain hidden here, the mist obscuring them easily.

Another night passed in cold silence as they waited for this group to reach its destination and praying that it was the right end. Soon, the rushing of the Idris broke through the mist from where it lay like a silver ribbon under the moonlight, its waters glimmering and dangerous. The voxis crossed at nightfall, making camp on the far banks. They watched as one by one they fell asleep before crossing and finding a place to wait until morning.

Two more days passed in a blur of glittering leaves and the sounds of the Singing Wood. The further they went, the more Lithia felt the fear mount. Cal had been with them for seven days, and until she laid eyes on a piece of gleaming opaline armor, she wouldn't be sure if this was the right way or not. In the silence, she began to question if she was wrong. To ask a hundred what-if questions that set her world spinning.

The trees themselves seemed to whisper to her that they knew the answers she was too blind to see. The second evening since they crossed the river, a clearing appeared before them, and Lithia's fear slammed into reality.

"We're here," Wil whispered. "Stay low."

They crouched beside a thick cluster of bushes, watching from the shadows as the voxis gathered around several large bonfires, their voices rising in greeting as the caravan arrived.

They couldn't just rush in, they weren't even sure if they were in the right place yet. The voxis were strong, and they were prepared for an ambush. Wil's eyes darted around the camp, her mind calculating the best course of action.

Lia's eyes narrowed as she scanned the perimeter. A ripple of dark energy seemed to swirl around the trees, and the hairs on the back of her neck stood on end. It wasn't just the voxis.

She let out a hard breath as she watched the large wraith that always lingered near her saunter into the group of gathered voxis. She barked something at the new arrivals, causing them to scatter. Several of them led her to the heavy wagon, uncovering it to reveal it laden with food and weapons.

The large fae flashed a vile grin before strutting back toward the tents. Wil jerked her head, and they began moving around the clearing, trying to track the wraith's progress through the camp. She wove between tents before ducking into the largest.

"We need to figure out where they have him," Lithia whispered.

Wil nodded. "We should wait for darkness to enter the clearing, but we need to circle the perimeter first to see what their defenses look like."

Lia nodded her agreement, and they began moving. As they came around the tents, another smaller fire came into view with several wraiths seated around it, looking weary in a way Lia hadn't expected.

And then, Lithia saw him.

Cal was bound to a large stone pillar just beyond the fire, his body battered and bruised. He was alive.

The thread in her heart hummed, and his eyes opened, locking with hers.

Calcas

Cal's body ached as he stirred awake, groggy, his vision blurry and mind thick with confusion. He had no idea how long he'd been unconscious, but the sharp tang of blood in the air and the harsh scent of smoke were enough to drag him out of the fog. His wrists were bound tightly above his head, his arms stretched out painfully, tethered to what felt like a cold, stone post. He took in shallow breaths, disoriented, trying to make sense of the world around him.

His head was pounding, a dull throb behind his eyes, and there was the sickening taste of iron on his tongue. He swallowed it back, shaking his head to clear the daze. But the movement only seemed to make it worse, intensifying the nauseous feeling roiling in his stomach.

His first clear thought: *Where am I?*

The sound of cracking fire and distant, muffled voices reached his ears, the rhythmic thumping of boots on hardened earth telling him he wasn't alone. He scanned the area, his vision still blurred.

The voxis.

How had he been taken by the voxis?

The memory came back in a rush, sharp and sudden. Seren's eyes, cold and unforgiving as she cut him off, every word she spoke slicing through him like a blade. He could still hear her voice echoing in his mind, the way she'd called him weak, the way she'd turned her back on everything they'd once stood for as she slashed at him. The blackness as he called out for Lia.

Cal tensed, trying to steady his breathing, but the sharp crack of a whip snapped him out of his thoughts.

He jerked his head up, catching a glimpse of movement outside the circle of firelight. She moved into the light, a feral smile curling her lips.

Seren's silhouette stood tall and proud in the dim light, her hair framed her face like a dark halo, and her golden eyes were fixed on him with such intensity it made his skin crawl.

"You're awake," she said, her voice soft, almost mocking. "*Good*. We can begin."

Cal's chest tightened, but he forced the words out. "Why?"

Her lips twisted into a smile, but there was no warmth. "Why?" she repeated. "Because you need to understand. You need to understand that there is no way out of this. No way back."

Her steps were deliberate as she approached him, and with each one, Cal's heart raced faster. He wasn't sure if it was from fear or anger, but he knew, with icy clarity, that this wasn't going to be an easy conversation. And she wasn't here to talk.

Her hand reached out, fingers brushing his cheek. He flinched away from the contact, his skin burning where she touched him. But Seren only laughed, the sound dark and taunting.

She murmured close to his ear. "You failed me, and now it's time for you to pay for that failure."

"I won't help you," he gritted out, his voice hoarse.

Her eyes flickered, narrowing, and with a sharp movement, she backhanded him across the face. The force of the strike was enough to make him reel, blood spilling from the split in his lip. But Seren didn't pause. She grabbed his jaw, forcing his face back to hers, her thumb pressing into the wound, twisting it.

"You don't have a choice," she spat. "You're going to help me, whether you like it or not. You'll help me bring down the veil, Calcas."

His breath came out in ragged gasps as he tried to turn his head away from her grip. But she was stronger. "I won't. I won't help you destroy everything."

Seren's expression darkened, and she stepped back, a cruel smirk curling on her lips. She motioned for someone to approach, and from the shadows, two others from The Hunt stepped forward, their faces concealed by helmets, but their intentions clear as one of them brandished a long, jagged blade. Cal's heart sank.

"You think your will alone is strong enough?" Seren asked, her voice laced with disdain. "The truth is, you're nothing without your friends. Without the hope you cling to. And you'll see that soon enough, once I've flayed it from your bones."

The wraith behind him pulled his head back, holding it in place with brutal force. Before Cal could inhale, the tip of the blade touched the skin of his throat, drawing a thin line of blood. His pulse hammered against the steel, each beat a countdown.

"Tell me," Seren said, her voice a whisper of silk, "How long before you beg?"

His breath was shallow, his heart hammering in his chest as the blade pressed harder against his throat. The room around him swirled in darkness, the echoes of his heartbeat drowning out everything else. He wanted to fight, wanted to lash out and scream at her, but he couldn't. Not like this.

But something inside him snapped. A spark of defiance, a flicker of the man he used to be. He swallowed hard and forced the words out.

"You'll never make me beg."

Seren's smile widened into something terrifying, and with a quick flick of her wrist, she motioned for the blade to be withdrawn.

She leaned in, her lips a breath from his. "I've made you beg before, Calcas, I can do it again," she murmured.

She shifted, and the knife made contact with his skin once more, as he gritted his teeth to choke down his screams.

Cal wasn't sure how long they tortured him. Time felt like a blur punctuated by blows, by forced silence, by the pressure of Seren's cold gaze on him at every turn. Each strike, each lash, each slice, was designed to break him. To force him to cave. But he wouldn't. He couldn't.

He thought of Lithia.

He thought of her face, her voice, the way her raw acceptance of all his flaws meant he could be more than what he was. She had made him believe that things could still be saved. He focused on the warmth of the thread in his chest and buried himself deep inside his mind.

But as the hours dragged on, his will began to weaken. His body screamed for mercy, but there was no mercy to be had. Seren's voice remained a constant, a low hum in the background of his suffering, reminding him that the longer he held out, the worse it would get.

"You'll break," she whispered once, leaning close to his ear, her breath cold against his skin. "And when you do, I will have you."

They want me to break, Cal thought, his mind swimming in a haze of pain. *But I can't. I won't.*

And somewhere deep within the fog of his thoughts, he heard Lithia's voice again. Soft, distant, but still there.

I love you, Cal. Don't let them drown you.

With a final, shuddering breath, Cal gritted his teeth and whispered to himself, "I won't give up."

They would have to break him themselves because he wasn't going to give them the satisfaction of seeing him beg.

It had been days, he had seen the moon several times, but it was a blur of unconsciousness.

He woke to the low murmur of conversation from where they sat in front of him, taunting him with the smell of their dinner. He closed his eyes, slumping back on the pillar, not wanting to attract their attention with the realization that he was awake when he felt it.

The thread in his chest gave a hum as if plucked.

His eyes popped open on instinct, locking with a set of depthless black eyes watching him from beyond the clearing.

LITHIA

L ia's pulse pounded in her throat as she crouched low behind the underbrush, her eyes never leaving Cal. Her heart pounded in her chest, drawn to him like a moth to a flame. He was broken, and she started to stand, needing to reach for him. A strong hand gripped her arm, holding her down, her mind snapping back into reality.

The clearing was mostly quiet aside from the crackling of the fire and the low murmurs of the wraiths who sat between their hiding spot and Cal's limp form. Their shadows danced in the flickering flame, attention entirely absorbed in their conversation, leaving the perimeter poorly guarded.

His eyes were locked onto hers, tired and haunted, and the world around her narrowed to the tiny sliver of space between them. Lia felt the thread in her chest throb with a steady pulse as they watched each other.

Cal's gaze flickered with fear as the wraiths laughed loudly in front of him, before he quickly masked it with a dull resignation. He knew better than to give any indication that he had seen her, that help was coming. His face remained neutral, but she could see the silent plea written in the tension of his body and the way his head finally sagged forward like a man near the edge of breaking.

Lia's breath hitched in her throat as she tore her eyes away from him, focusing on Wil. The two of them had trained for the kind of quiet, deadly movements that would slip under the radar of even the most vigilant eyes. Wil was scanning the area, her face a mask of concentration, spymaster indeed.

Wil's eyes flicked toward Lia, her fingers making a subtle gesture that indicated a plan was forming.

Lia nodded once, her heart racing as Wil began to move.

The clearing was large, filled with scattered tents and the glow of campfires. The voxis were spread out in small groups, some talking, others sharpening blades or cleaning their armor. No one seemed particularly alert, but there were still too many to risk charging in, especially with Seren's dark presence hanging like a storm cloud above them and no sure idea of where she was.

Wil crept toward the far edge of the clearing, where the trees thickened as a heavy mist crept like fingers around the trunks before a storm. Their place in the thicket placed them as close as they could get to Cal. Its glaring disadvantage being that, coming from behind him, he would have no warning when they moved.

The minutes felt like hours as the fire crackled, sending shadows that danced grotesquely over the voxis's faces as they moved between fires. The few wraiths they had seen had kept to the single fire near Cal for the entire day, taunting him and beating him in turn. Finally, after what seemed like an eternity, the camp quieted as the moon rose higher in the sky. The last of the wraiths finally headed to their tents, their footsteps muffled in the soft earth.

"Fucking finally," Wil bit out, startling Lia.

Lia moved first, her steps silent as she slid between the trees. Wil followed, merging seamlessly into the night. The sound of their movements was blotted out by the soft whisper of wind through the leaves, and the swirling mist blurred them in the darkness outside the firelight.

They circled in toward the fire, eyes trained for the slightest movement, every step deliberate. Lia's gaze darted between the lingering voxis who remained milling around distant tents. As they got closer, they realized not all of the wraiths had left. The largest of the wraiths, the one who enjoyed berating Lia, was sitting just a few paces from the stone pillar where Cal was bound. Her eyes, glowing faintly in the dim light, were focused on the fire.

But this was their chance.

Wil continued ahead, her form blending into the shadows like liquid smoke, her eyes narrowed and every muscle tensed for action. Lia stayed low, her heart pounding in her ears.

They were just a few feet from the pillar now, the stone looming ahead of them. Cal's body was slumped against it, his head bowed, his arms straining against rough, iron shackles. His chest rose and fell in shallow, pained breaths.

Lia's heart clenched as she stepped closer. She could see the blood—so much blood—staining his clothes, his face bruised and battered. Her fingers tingled with the desire to reach out, to touch him, to feel the warmth of his skin, to reassure him that she was here. But she couldn't risk it.

A grunt and snap of movement, and Lia froze, her eyes snapping toward the wraith. She stood abruptly, stretching her long limbs. She walked slowly toward the fire, muttering to herself. Wil's hand caught Lia's wrist, steadying her as they both held their breath. She passed within a few feet of them, her eyes only once straying from the fire to land on Cal before stalking away.

When she was safely out of sight, Wil exhaled, her grip relaxing.

Lia didn't wait any longer. She moved in quickly, stepping out of the shadows and crossing the short distance between her and Cal.

He looked up at her in disbelief, his eyes wide with recognition. His lips parted as if to speak, but no sound came out.

"We're getting you out of here. Will you be able to move?" she whispered, her voice hoarse but full of certainty.

His gaze flicked to the shackles around his wrists, then back to her. His expression softened, but his eyes were filled with an ocean of pain. He tried to speak again, but the words caught in his throat.

Lia reached out, gently running a trembling thumb along a deep purple bruise on his jaw before she fumbled with the cold iron around his wrists. No key. No time.

With a sharp breath, she looked to Wil, who nodded, wrapping a dark hand around the iron.

The air hummed, the faint pulse of power rippled, setting her hair on end. It was the faintest touch, just enough to make the iron buckle, but it worked. The metal groaned under the pressure, twisting and cracking as it yielded.

Cal's arms fell heavy to his side, and he gritted his teeth in pain.

"Cal, love, I'm so sorry," she whispered, her voice shaking now. "But we don't have much time. We need to go. Now."

He winced, his body trembling as he slowly shifted his weight. "Lia...I..." His words faltered, his face pale and drawn, but the relief in his eyes was unmistakable.

Lia's heart twisted painfully. "I know," she smiled. "But we're getting you out of here. I won't leave you behind."

Before he could respond, they froze at the crackle of a twig.

A voice, low and menacing, came from behind them. "Mmm, little mice in the woods seem to have chewed through your chains, Calcas."

Lia's breath caught in her lungs. She whirled to find the wraith from earlier, now standing just a few feet away, her dark eyes gleaming with malice.

The wraith raised her hand, the air around her crackling with magic.

"Get behind me," Wil hissed.

Lia's heart dropped. This wasn't supposed to happen. They had to move now.

"Run," she urged Cal. "We'll hold her off!"

But Cal's eyes, suddenly sharp and full of resolve, locked on her.

"No," he said, his voice strong despite the exhaustion and pain.

The wraith's lips curled into a smile. "How brave...How very...very...stupid."

The charge of imminent danger crackled through the clearing. And as the wraith's body shot forward toward them, Lia closed her syphon on the thread of rotted magic in her core and pulled.

LITHIA

The wraith fell with a strangled cry, clutching her chest. It wasn't like the necsite; she didn't have a life force to snuff out, instead Lia was simply strangling her magic.

The clearing erupted into chaos.

Lia's heart raced as she twisted her wrist, forcing the rotten thread of magic to writhe under her control. The wraith struggled to her feet, struggling to keep her balance.

A pulse of magic shot past Lia, slamming into the wraith with so much force that it sent a shockwave through the trees. The wraith screeched, staggering back, but only for a moment. It was like trying to stop a storm with a breath as she came for them again.

Wil was already moving, blade drawn, her face set in a mask of grim determination. She lunged forward to intercept the wraith's retaliatory strike, her body a blur. Lia watched the exchange, a swift clash of steel, the wraith's rage fueled strikes grazing Wil's armor like whispers of death. But Wil never flinched.

"Cal, we have to move," Lia urged again, pushing him forward, her chest constricting. His battered form staggered, but he obeyed, pushing off the stone pillar with a grunt of pain. He was slow...so slow...but his jaw was set as he dragged himself along.

"Go, Lia! Now!" Wil shouted, her sword clashing with the wraith's dark magic in a burst of sparks.

Lia grabbed Cal's arm and pulled him toward the treeline, toward the safety of the mist-draped forest. His legs wobbled with every step, his breath shallow and ragged, but he moved.

Behind them, Wil took the brunt of the wraith's fury. Wil punched out toward her chest, and the wraith's form flickered. Lia froze, trying to catch up with the scene playing out in front of her as Wil pulled her hand back and the wraith dissolved into smoke.

Wil turned to follow them, her eyes flat as they continued to crash through the underbrush, the trees groaning in the wind as they left the clearing behind.

Cal's breathing was labored, his entire body trembling from the combined pain and exhaustion. But the thread of magic that bound him to Lia pulsed steadily, like a heartbeat.

Wil grabbed her arm as they moved, steering her along the perimeter of the clearing. Lithia could feel the confusion as it painted her features. They continued for several minutes before coming up on the small paddock filled with horses.

"Damn it," Lia cursed. "They're right on us."

She turned to glance back, eyes catching the flash of steel as a wraith stalked through the brush searching for their trail. Lia's pulse hammered in her temples as she snapped her gaze back to the paddock. The horses were already spooked, their eyes wide with fear, ears twitching at the distant sounds of their pursuers hunting them.

"We're not going to make it on foot," Wil muttered, already heading toward the nearest horse, a sleek bay mare that was nervously stamping the ground. "They're closing in."

"I wish we had thought of it earlier and had them waiting," Lia snapped, the words jagged edged. She should have had a better plan, but her mind felt so clouded.

Wil shook her head. "No, we needed to be able to release all of them so they can't follow," she said, voice soft with understanding. "Come on."

Cal stumbled forward, barely keeping up with them, his breath coming in ragged gasps. Lia's heart twisted. She glanced at Wil, who was crouching to help lift Cal onto the largest horse.

"You ride with him," she urged. "We'll outrun them."

Lia slung herself up in front of Cal as the mare snorted, her hooves thudding heavily against the earth. Lia's heart lurched as she watched Wil mount and ride toward the gate. She opened it wide, circling back to Lia and Cal before sending a burst of magic rolling along the ground.

The already anxious animals startled and stampeded toward the gate, the three of them joining the flow until they broke free in the cover of the forest.

The horses were at a full gallop now, hooves pounding the dirt and rattling the branches overhead. The air was cold, wind and branches whipping her face, and Lia could feel the weight of every second ticking down.

Wil pulled near her and yelled over the thunder, "They'll be tracking us. They know who we are, so we just need to outrun them and make it to Arachin."

Lia's gaze darted around the Singing Wood, the unsettling feeling of being hunted leaching into her bones. Cal was limp at her back but holding tight to her waist. She turned her head to try to see him. His face was pale, his eyes squeezed tight in pain.

They rode hard through the night, their horses tearing through the dense underbrush.

A screech split the air.

Lia's heart stuttered.

"They're gaining on us!" Lia choked, looking over her shoulder to see the wraith's gleaming armor flickering between the trees, too close for comfort.

Wil cursed, a crow swooped overhead.

"Go left!" Wil shouted suddenly. "We are nearly to the bridge, it doesn't matter if we use the road, it will be faster!"

Lia didn't hesitate. She veered sharply left, tearing through the thick underbrush for several more minutes before bursting out onto the road.

As soon as they hit the clear road, she urged her mare faster, its heavy hoofbeats echoing through the sleeping wood. Wil crashed out onto the road a few moments later, and they rode toward the edge of the forest, the glittering lights of the Infernum Bridge popping up through the trees.

The moment they broke through the trees, the fae stationed at the bridge fort were able to see them, alarm bells sounding and sentinels pouring across the roofline. The wide doors began to open in the distance, and she let out a hard breath as another shriek echoed from the treeline.

They barreled through the gates, pulling to a stop to find Neda barking orders at the gathered sentinels to close the gate quickly and Tadhg waiting anxiously, his eyes locked on Cal. Wil dismounted quickly, and Tadhg helped her pull Cal from his place behind Lia, laying him in a small cart as Lia slid off the mare.

Tadhg jumped into the back of the cart with Cal, his hands drifting over him for several minutes before they began to glow.

Neda stepped up beside her. "They are watching the forest, but I don't think they intend to follow you. Come on, let's get him to the Citadel before Astris comes all the way down here to kill me."

Lia started walking, and Neda put a hand on her shoulder. "Get in the fucking cart, Lia."

Calcas

The cart jostled violently over a rut in the bridge, and Cal felt his world shatter into a thousand splinters of pain.

He didn't scream.

There was no strength left in him to scream.

A low, guttural sound escaped him—half gasp, half sob—but even that was swallowed by the roar of blood in his ears. His body had become a map of agony, every joint an open wound, every breath a challenge. A fire had taken root in his ribs and spine, and it burned hotter with every movement, every bump of the wheels on stone.

The world around him was a blur. The pale crescent of the moon wheeled high above, filtering silver light through the clouds that clung to the stars as they blinked down with cold indifference.

He squeezed his eyes shut to combat the rising nausea as the world spun.

His wrists had been rubbed raw, open, and swollen. He could still feel the cruel shape of the manacles even though they were gone, still felt the bite of metal each time he twitched.

His lips were cracked, blood crusted at the corners of his mouth. He could feel the bruises that bloomed over every inch of his skin, but it was the wounds beneath, the ones that didn't bleed, that threatened to unravel him.

But there was one constant.

Lia's hand.

It was warm and heavy...and shaking in his own, and it grounded him more than the wagon, more than Tadhg's healing magic, more than the looming walls of the Citadel they were fast approaching. Her thumb brushed over the back of his hand in steady circles, like she was reminding him he was still here. Still real.

The pressure of her touch was the only thing tethering him to the world.

His eyelids fluttered open, and everything swam in front of him again. The light from the lanterns bobbed ahead. The silhouettes of riders on either side. The faint gold glow of magic came from Tadhg's hands as he crouched beside him. The pain was so thick it blurred the faces, bent the voices around him. But he knew her.

She leaned over him, her face carved with worry, eyes wide and red-rimmed.

"Lia," he rasped, the word breaking like glass in his throat.

Her face came closer, hovering just above his own. "I'm here," she said, voice raw. "I have you. Just hold on."

He tried to nod. The pain said no.

"I didn't forget you," he whispered. "They tried. Gods, she tried to make me forget you."

The words dragged themselves from the pit of him, splintered and jagged and too honest.

Lia stared down at him, tears breaking free to roll down her face.

Cal's eyes fluttered again, gaze unfocused. "There were moments I...I didn't know who I was. Didn't know what was real. But you were...always there. In the dark. Just out of reach."

"I was reaching too."

A tear fell from her lashes and landed on his face. Her hand trembled as she wiped it away. He leaned into it instinctively, eyes closing with a faint sound that wasn't quite relief, but the closest he could manage.

"They didn't want information," he said, after a long pause. "It wasn't that. They didn't ask questions. They didn't care about strategy or secrets or names."

Lia swallowed. "Then what did they want?"

He blinked up at her, and there was nothing in her eyes as she built up her walls, awaiting an answer she already expected.

"They wanted to hollow me out," he said quietly. "Seren...she said that...that hope made me weak."

A shudder rolled through him.

"I thought she might be right," he whispered. "I thought...maybe if I stopped hoping, it would hurt less."

Lia's fingers curled around his hand tightly. "She failed."

Silence fell between them for a moment, but it wasn't empty.

Lia shifted closer, until her forehead rested gently against his. "You can let yourself be cracked and broken. We'll make something new out of the pieces. But I'm not letting you disappear. Not ever again."

Tadhg's magic surged at that moment, heat blooming along Cal's ribs, knitting tissue together. It didn't erase the damage, but it gave him just enough space to breathe again.

He gasped, and this time, the breath didn't taste like iron.

The cart rattled as it reached the Citadel gates, the sounds of steel grating open and urgent voices rising to meet them.

Lanterns flared.

Footsteps rushed forward.

He didn't register most of it.

Because as they lifted him from the cart, blinding pain tore through his body, and all he could do was watch her.

She stayed by his side as they carried him through the familiar archways, past old doors and pale-glowing lanterns. The wards to the private wings buzzed gently, washing over him like a breeze through an open window. Comforting. Familiar.

They lowered him onto a wide bed, and Lia's familiar scent washed over him as Tadhg settled over him once more. He heard several quiet voices and shifting movements in the room around him, but he only stared at the stone of the ceiling.

Hissing between her teeth at the state of his torso, he recognized his mother's voice for the first time. She bustled around him, undressing him and following Tadhg's quiet instruction as she applied a thick green paste that burned against his skin as it touched an open lash mark. He bit down on a scream that threatened to rise.

Lia still hadn't let go.

Her hand was there, even when his body arched in pain. Even when his breath stuttered and tears slipped silently down his cheeks, her hand never left his.

He turned his head toward her, blinking against the light. His voice was barely a whisper.

"Please don't go."

"I'm not going anywhere," she said. "I'll stay beside you until the sky crumbles and the mountains fall into the sea."

His voice broke on the next words, as quiet and raw as a confession. "She almost made me beg."

"You wouldn't be any less if you had," Lia whispered, brushing the hair from his forehead.

He let out a sound that was almost a sob, almost a laugh.

And then, finally, his body sagged into the bed as sleep tugged at him like a tide.

Before he let go, he held her gaze and whispered the words he'd clung to through every whip-crack and blade.

"I love you, little dragon."

Her fingers pressed to his lips gently, reverently.

"And I love you, Cal," she said, fierce and unwavering. "Even threadbare. Even broken. Right where you are."

As the magic wrapped around him and the pain dulled to a distant hum, he let the darkness take him.

LITHIA

She woke with a start, her head heavy, disoriented. She blinked, trying to clear the fog in her mind, the edges of her thoughts still blurring with the remnants of fear and exhaustion. She was over-warm and wrapped in heavy blankets, and it took her several groggy minutes to remember she was back in her own bed for the first time since they left for Thahaos's temple weeks ago.

Her eyes adjusted to the dim firelight spilling across the room. At first, it was just shadows, the flicker of flame casting long lines of light across the stone walls, but then—Cal.

Lia's heart gave a jolt.

He lay beside her, his face a dark map of bruises. His chest rose and fell in shallow, steady breaths, the rhythmic rise and fall a quiet comfort to her frantic mind. His deeper wounds were now hidden beneath bandages, but the memory of his pain when they had arrived was fresh, clawing at the edges of her thoughts. His broken form, his bloodied hands, the raw fear in his eyes when he whispered her name. But in the soft stillness of the room, it seemed like the world had paused, waiting for them.

It was Tadhg's voice that broke through the silence. "He is strong, Lia. It will just take a little longer. His body just needs rest."

Lia turned to him, her eyes locking with the healer's. His expression was warm and she saw the faint flicker of his own concern before he shuffled it aside to smile at her.

"Thank you." Lia's voice was hoarse.

Tadhg nodded, a small, reassuring smile settling at the corner of his lips. "He'll be fine. But you...you're not. You're wound tighter than a drum, but I know you aren't likely to listen to me if I tell you to rest."

Lia opened her mouth to protest, but Tadhg held up a hand. "I'll go with you. I understand why you can't rest and why it can't wait any longer. I already sent word back to the high priestess this morning that we would be there as soon as you woke up."

Her shoulders relaxed; she had expected him to argue, to get the others to push as well, but he proved to her time and again that he knew her better than anyone.

"Let's go then. I don—I don't know what is going to happen when I take on the final shard." She chewed her lip.

Tadhg's smile slipped some. "I will be there to catch you if you fall, Mo Bhanrighit."

He bowed deeply before turning and closing the door.

Lia stood up slowly, the room tilting as she pushed against the dizziness that threatened to take her. She looked down at Cal's sleeping form, his features softened, and kissed him softly on the nose.

"I'll be back soon," she said, though her voice faltered at the end.

The morning was colder than she expected as she walked down the streets of Arachin beside Tadhg. When she had dressed that morning, she felt wrong strapping weapons to her body to enter the temple, so all she wore was the sword of Mab. It felt fitting that the weapon that was there when the magic was shattered would be there when it was reforged.

The city was still quiet below as they trudged up the rose quartz steps of the temple in the blue light of predawn. As they reached the doors, they swung open on silent hinges to reveal the faceless High Priestess waiting for them.

"Welcome home, Mo Bhanrighit," she said in her measured tone. "Tell me what you need from us."

Lithia smiled weakly as she spoke.

"I need you to take us to that chamber we trained in with my syphon magic. I can explain as we walk."

The priestess tilted her head slightly but stepped to the side, gesturing them in quickly.

As they made their way down the narrow halls and stairs, Lithia told the High Priestess everything that had happened and explained their belief that the final piece of Suviel's heart was here below the temple. By the time they stepped onto the damp stone floor of the cave, the High Priestess was muttering to herself.

Lithia took in the beauty of the room, examining all she could see for any indication of where the shard would be.

She closed her eyes to take a steadying breath and found herself feeling for the threads of magic in the room like she would in the poppies. She ran her fingers through glittering strands of magic as she tumbled over places in the small cave that could hide the shard when a blinding light filled her senses.

She ran her hands through the magic again until she found the blinding white thread. Hesitantly, she reached out to touch it, just to see what it was, when she was violently thrown back into reality.

She opened her eyes as her back hit the wall to find a look of shock on Tadhg's face. Frantically scanning the room, she saw what his eyes locked onto. On the wall where the Goddess walked through the world, right where Aduna's heart would be, the mosaic tiles began to fall away. One by one, they fell, shattering as they struck the floor. In their place, bursting from Aduna's chest, was white light.

The tiles continued to fall, revealing the entirety of the shard in Aduna's place in the mosaic. Lia looked at the others and found Tadhg smiling grimly and the High Priestess on her knees facing up into the magic.

Lithia moved toward the wall, her heart pounding in her chest. The shard, now fully revealed, shimmered with an ethereal brilliance that seemed to hum with the same ancient power that filled her chest.

Lia reached out, her fingertips brushing the cool surface of the magic.

This is it, she thought. *This is where it all ends.*

But as her hand pressed into the shard, the rush of power she had expected did not come. There was no surge, no flash of light. No overwhelming flood of magic.

Instead, the shard was cold. Silent. Still.

Her breath hitched, confusion lapping at the edges of her mind. It felt...empty. Like a hollow vessel waiting for something that never came. The silence in the chamber stretched, thick with the weight of their collective confusion. Her heart raced, a sense of unease settling deep in her bones.

"This can't be it," Lia muttered, frustration bubbling up inside her. "There has to be more. There *has* to be."

She closed her eyes and exhaled slowly.

And in the stillness, she finally felt it.

The magic inside the shard *stirred*, just a breath, just a whisper, and then it began to shift. The coldness melted away, replaced by something softer, warmer.

It wasn't a flood, but a slow, steady flow. A current that ran through her veins, calming, steadying. It wasn't like the other shards, which had surged like a storm, wild and untamable. This was different. This was controlled, tempered, as if it had always been a part of her.

Lia opened her eyes. The magic glowed brighter not with blinding light, but with a gentle, pulsing glow, like the steady beat of a heart.

The weight of it all hit her at once, but instead of overwhelming her, it felt like the final piece of the puzzle slotting into place. The glow dulled as the magic settled, and she looked around, expecting...something.

But nothing came.

She could feel all the shards still separate, but within her. She opened her mouth to express her confusion when the world began to shake.

LITHIA

Debris fell from the ceiling as the temple rocked above them. Lia's heart lodged in her throat as her eyes blew wide, locking with Tadhg's. They stood frozen for less than a breath before a loud boom rocked the ground again, chunks of the cave walls falling into the clear water.

They bolted for the door, Tadhg pulling the High Priestess into motion. They stumbled up the narrow stairs as the temple vibrated around them, a loud crack sounding as the tunnel below them collapsed.

They burst into the hall, leaving the High Priestess to calm the trembling acolytes cowering in the hall. As they skidded around the end of the hall into the large atrium, an ear-splitting screech filled the space, rippling the water of the large pool and causing all the fae around the room to clutch at their ears.

Writhing through the jagged hole it had made in the stone was a glittering black amphiptere, its wings stirring the dust and rubble from its destruction. Atop the creature sat Seren.

The first light of the day cut across her, gilding her like the early morning mountains. Her golden eyes were hard, merciless. She looked like death crowned, but she wasn't. Lia could see in her depths the fear of life moving on without her, driving her to madness. Thahaos had been wrong to allow her to watch life unfold so soon after her death. It had been a cruel decision.

Lia's breath caught, the pain in her chest eclipsed by the fury at how many lives she had taken for foolish vengeance.

Seren smiled. Slowly. Mockingly.

"Took you long enough," she purred, voice echoing unnaturally off the temple stones. "Did you get lost in the dark, little queen? Or were you simply too weak to make it out?"

Tadhg bristled beside her. "We weren't expecting to need to greet Thahaos's bitch so early in the morning."

Seren rolled her eyes and slid from the amphiptere's back with inhuman grace. Her boots kissed the stone and the sound reverberated through the air like a clap of thunder.

"How crass." She tilted her head toward Lia. "How is he? He broke so beautifully. You should be proud."

Lia's fingers closed around the hilt of Mab's sword.

"You're lying, Ser. You know he is not broken."

Seren descended the rubble like a queen in her court. Her amphiptere shifted behind her, its serpentine body curling protectively, glowing eyes fixed on Lia, unblinking.

"Am I?" Seren asked, her tone light, too light. "You forged nothing. You have left the heart incomplete. You're still half a weapon. Dull."

Lia stepped forward. "You took him because you knew we were close."

Seren's expression sharpened. "No," she said. "I took him because *you* never deserved him. Because watching you both crumble after you rejected me..."

Tadhg moved to block her path, his blade half-drawn. "Enough. This isn't a council chamber. You don't get to talk your way out of this."

But Lia raised a hand, stopping him.

She walked forward, slow, controlled, until she stood a few steps from Seren.

"You have lost Seren," Lia said, her voice low.

Seren laughed, the sound raw and feral. "Oh, you don't really think that, do you, Lithia? Not when you failed again. Not when your magic flickers instead of roars."

Her blade sang as it left its sheath.

Lia barely raised hers in time. The first clash sent a shockwave through the air, sparking light across the dusk-shadowed temple.

Steel met steel, magic flared, and the amphiptere reared, wings buffeting the air in great, thundering gusts.

Her blade danced with shadow. Lia struggled to match her, drawing on every lesson, every instinct. She moved on adrenaline, her body screaming with fatigue, but her will unbroken.

Seren feinted, then slashed. Lia ducked just in time, the impact jarring her arm to the elbow.

"You can't win," Seren hissed, their faces inches apart. "You still haven't forged the Heart. You're nothing but dust."

Lia shoved her back as she channeled the shard of magic still clinging to her core, letting it flare outward in a sudden surge. Mab's blade ignited with threads of flame and night.

The force pushed Seren and Lithia apart, leaving them both stumbling and disoriented.

The amphiptere shrieked.

The beast leaped from its perch, barreling toward them with talons outstretched. Lia raised her blade, the magic flared outward uncontrolled, and slammed a wave into its flank, sending it crashing into a pillar.

The temple groaned, stones fracturing.

Seren snarled, rage twisting her features as she regained her footing. Blood dripped from her lip where one of Lia's strikes had found its mark. "This isn't over," she spat.

And with a whistle sharp enough to split bone, she turned, leaping onto the amphiptere's back as it wobbled in pain and rose into the sky.

The temple cracked beneath their feet.

Tadhg touched her shoulder, kneeling beside her. "We have to move. The temple is collapsing."

Lia looked to the sky, where smoke swallowed the last glint of Seren's retreat.

She turned to Tadhg as he gestured wildly to the gathered fae hiding in the alcoves.

"Go! Move! Out, now!"

She followed his lead and ran to the far side of the room, clearing the alcoves there and ordering everyone out of the groaning temple.

The High Priestess ran up behind them at the back of the game group from the hall, shooing them out the doors.

"I believe that is everyone we need to go."

The temple gave another groan as large chunks began to fall from the ceiling.

They fled down the temple stairs in a wild sprint, the steps trembling beneath their feet. Halfway down, a final, deafening roar echoed behind them, and with a heart-wrenching *crash*, the top of the temple gave way, the great domed roof splintering and collapsing in a shower of stone. It plunged into Soundless Bay.

LITHIA

The wind clawed at Lia's skin as they stumbled away from the broken temple, her legs struggling to carry her weight. Her body screamed with exhaustion, but her magic churned violently beneath her skin, a boiling current she couldn't contain. It surged up her spine, crawling under her ribs and pooling like molten iron in her chest.

Every heartbeat was a thunderclap. Every breath set her nerves on fire. She gritted her teeth to keep from crying out, but the magic was slipping through the cracks in her control. It was too much.

Tadhg stayed close, his expression tight with worry, eyes flicking nervously between her and the path ahead. They descended the scorched slope in silence, the temple still groaning behind them, unsettled by the violence Seren left in her wake. Grit and ash clung to their skin, and the air itself seemed to buzz with aftershocks.

Lia stumbled. The world tilted.

Another spike of magic ripped through her, unbidden. Her vision flared white. Her hand twitched violently at her side, and the ground beneath her feet cracked open with a sound like bone breaking. The scent of scorched earth filled the air.

"Lia," Tadhg said quietly, fear threading through his voice. His hand hovered near her arm, unsure what kind of help she needed.

She didn't look at him. "I'm fine," she lied. "We need to get back."

But she wasn't fine. Not even close.

They ran unsteadily through the city. The buildings were blurring as the residents of Arachin stepped out into the streets to the new skyline and wails of loss. Every step sent new pulses of pain through Lia's body. Her hands trembled, wrapped in glittering black magic. Her thoughts fractured like glass, and whispers of magic needled into her mind.

The Citadel loomed ahead of them like the eye of a storm, still and quiet. The sight of it should have brought comfort. Instead, it only reminded her of how close she was to losing control entirely.

When they finally arrived, the gates opened without ceremony, guards stepping aside as sentinels streamed past them toward the temple. No words were spoken. The tension that coiled in the air around them was suffocating.

Neda met them in the courtyard, her face pale, mouth tight with barely contained alarm.

"You look like hell," she said flatly. But her voice trembled, betraying the fear she tried to mask. Her eyes darted between Lia's, a clash of green and black.

Her knees buckled.

Another surge of magic clawed up her spine. It seized her lungs, strangled her breath. Her vision doubled. She bit her lip until she tasted blood to keep from screaming as white fire licked along her fingertips. Her hands sparked uncontrollably, and the air around her warped.

Tadhg caught her arm. "Lia!"

She jerked away, gasping. "I'm fine. Just—get me inside. Now."

They guided her through the winding halls of the Citadel. Every step was agony. Her body felt like it was being pulled apart at the seams. Her magic refused to settle, flaring with every heartbeat, sparking dangerously in her palms. Passing staff flattened themselves against walls, watching her with wide eyes, murmuring prayers under their breath.

She could hear the fear in their silence. See it in the way they wouldn't meet her gaze. Her footsteps left behind scorched prints on the ancient stone.

Wil was waiting in Lia's study, a map unrolled before her, ink still drying, dark circles carved beneath her eyes like bruises. She looked up as they entered, her gaze falling immediately on Lia, and going sharp.

She snapped up. "What happened?"

"We found the shard," Lia rasped, voice raw. "Seren came…" She panted. "We fought…She ran."

Tadhg continued, "The magic, Lia took it on but…" He glanced at her before he continued, "But something didn't work right, or there is something else that needs to be done because it seems to still be broken pieces. But Seren showed up and broke the top off the temple, so we didn't get to discuss it much."

Wil didn't ask for more. She crossed the room quickly and helped Lia to a chair. The wood creaked under her weight like even the furniture feared her. The air thickened with a strange charge, like lightning waiting to strike.

Wil turned to the others, her voice taut. "I received word this morning. From my mother. I had come here to find you."

Tadhg knelt beside Lia, his brows pinched as he ran glowing hands over her. Neda stepped closer.

"Some of the wraiths in The Beneath have defected," Wil said. Her voice was low, but each word landed like a blow. "They've joined Seren. They're helping her tear at the Veil."

Lia's breath caught. Ice wrapped around her ribs. Her hands clenched the arms of the chair, trembling.

"They've already begun," Wil continued. "There are cracks now. Small ones. But my mother says the Veil is fraying. Fast. And when it breaks…"

She didn't finish.

Lia hissed in a breath, "Why would they?"

Wil shook her head. "From what her letter said, they are all first wraiths, the ones created in the beginning by Thahaos. I'm not sure what motive they would have besides power. I do fear it is my fault, though." She closed her eyes. "When we were rescuing Cal…I…I sent that wraith back to The Beneath. I assumed my father would find her immediately, but it appears she was able to recruit instead."

Another pulse of magic slammed through Lia like a hammer to the spine. Her body convulsed. Her breath hitched. Fire exploded from her fingertips in a violent burst. The map on the table ignited instantly, curling to ash as smoke billowed upward.

Tadhg yelped and jumped away from her.

"Lia!" Wil barked, eyes wide.

"I can't—" she gasped, clutching at her chest. "I can't hold it back!"

Her vision swam. Her skin burned from within, every nerve screaming. She lurched from the chair, her legs tangling beneath her. Shadows leaked from her fingertips like oil. Her magic had become something foreign, violent…alive.

"Get away from me!" she cried. "I can feel it breaking me!"

Tadhg reached for her, but a shockwave burst from her body, knocking him back. A final, violent surge of magic burst from her chest in a wave of shadow and fire. The walls groaned. Shelves cracked. Books flew like birds scattering in a storm. Wil threw up a barrier of darkness just in time to shield them.

Lia screamed. Not just in pain, but in helpless rage. The sound tore through the room, raw and hollow, echoing back like the cries of a collapsing world.

And then, everything went black.

CALCAS

Cal woke to the scent of fire.

Not the clean crackle of a hearth or the wild blaze of a battlefield. No, this fire was wrong. Acrid and sour. It filled his nose and lungs and coated his tongue. It tasted like ruin. Like grief.

He gasped, sitting up too fast. His limbs trembled. Every joint ached like he'd been nailed to the floor and left to rot. The world came into focus slowly, framed by the soft green linens of Lithia's bed. Light filtered in through high windows, fracturing into a million colors through the stained glass. The air was too still.

Magic lingered here. Thick. Smothering. He could feel it like pressure behind his eyes, a fading hum crawling across his skin.

Something was very, very wrong.

The room was empty, save for the healer's tools and a tray of untouched herbs. A familiar stack of blades and weapons rested on the table beside the bed. Not his. *Hers.*

His breath hitched. He threw off the blanket and swung his legs over the edge, his body groaning in protest. Pain bit through his skull like a rusted spike. Memories came in flashes: the labyrinth, Seren's voice, escaping, the wagon, Lia kissing his nose—

Lia.

He staggered to his feet, catching the edge of the table for balance. Magic sparked around his fingertips and fizzled out. He wasn't whole. Not yet. But he was enough.

He stepped into the study.

He took in a shattered window, its frame scorched and warped. A tapestry half-consumed by fire. The smell of burned parchment and melted metal hit him first. Then the magic struck, like walking into a storm. Chaotic and alive.

Then he saw her.

Lia lay on the floor, wrapped in blankets, unconscious. Her hair freeing itself from her braid at all angles like a crown of wildfire. Her skin glowed faintly like her veins were backlit by lightning. Tadhg sat slumped against the far wall, a gash stitched across his temple, hands bruised. Wil sat with Lithia's head resting in her lap, her mouth set in a hard line.

She looked up when she saw Cal. Her eyes widened with something like relief and fear.

"You're awake," she said softly.

"What happened to her?"

Tadhg stirred. "She took on the last shard. But it's unstable. She's not controlling it. It's...It's controlling her."

"Why would she go alone that wa–" Wil's expression cut him off. Her eyes narrowed at Tadhg. He shifted course. "Did it not work then?"

Wil shook her head.

"It worked, she has all five pieces of the heart, but they seem to still be separate pieces. I'm not sure what that means. Are there more out there, or do we just need to find a way to fix it?"

Cal stepped closer, ignoring the pain flaring in his chest. Lia was still. Too still. Magic bled off her skin in twitching waves, flickering and volatile. It repelled him and begged for him all at once. He could feel the echo of her heartbeat, wild and erratic.

He knelt beside her.

"She thought she could contain it," Wil continued quietly. "But the veil is tearing. Seren has help now while Lia's...burning from the inside out."

Cal swallowed hard. "She's going to die."

"Not if we find a way to reforge the heart, we need to find a way to knit the magic back together," Wil said. But even she sounded uncertain. Her voice shook, just enough to betray how close to the line was.

Cal brushed his hand just above Lia's cheek. Her skin shimmered with power. A low hum thrummed against his bones. He could feel the pain she wasn't awake to voice. It was a storm in her blood, clawing to be freed.

And then Wil's words hit him.

The Fateweaver.

He had gone in desperation. Alone. Foolish.

But the Fateweaver hadn't spoken of the mate bond. Not explicitly. They had spoken of *threads*. Of fate choosing. Of the weave of magic itself. And a weaver, being one who could mend, one who sat outside time and watched the loom.

He looked at Wil. "Could the fateweaver fix it?"

"I...I don't know. It's possible that if they can't themself fix it that they know who could. The weaver is older than I am and has seen many threads of magic."

Cal nodded. "I went to them once, I think...I think I went to them because fate knew I would need them again, just not for any reason I believed I would."

Wil frowned. "You went to them? Why would you risk that?"

"Because I thought...it doesn't matter anymore, it was long ago before the battle in the valley," Cal said. "And now...I think I may be understanding what they said for the first time."

Wil eyed him with suspicion as he rubbed soft circles on Lia's hand.

"Fae generally do not leave the weaver with the result they expected. What did they tell you?"

He sighed. "'The one I love wasn't the one fate chose, but fate chose the one I love. Until right now, I assumed they were talking about the mate bond choosing Lia when I believed I loved Seren but—" He played the entire interaction with the fateweaver over in his head. "They knew I would say no..."

Wil stared at him unblinking.

He stood, voice steadying as he felt the threads of his own fate coming together. "We need to go. Now. Before she fractures beyond repair."

Behind him, Lia twitched in her sleep, slowly blinking her eyes open.

"If she wakes like this again," Tadhg said hoarsely, "we might not survive the next outburst."

Cal looked down at her, guilt and love and fear warring in his chest. He took her hand despite the heat and the pulse of magic that warned him away.

"Hold on, Lia," he whispered. "We are almost there."

CALCAS

Then

The Fate Weaver's cabin was a twisted thing, half-grown into the side of an ancient elm, the bark and walls indistinguishable in the moonlight. The forest around it held its breath, the silence absolute. Even the insects knew better than to sing here.

Cal stood on the threshold, drenched in sweat despite the cold, hand hovering above the crooked door.

He hadn't told Lia or Seren.

He couldn't.

They would never understand—why he would come here, to this place.

But Cal had felt the bond in his chest tightening each day, a thread strung too taut between their souls. It was beautiful and damning. It made him ache in ways no wound ever had.

The door swung open.

Inside, the air was thick with incense. Ribbons of spider-silk laced through rafters. Glowing threads hung like veins from the ceiling, each one pulsing softly in different hues, green, silver, crimson. Lives and fates, woven into something monstrous and divine.

The fateweaver sat hunched over a loom that glowed with spectral light. Their face was obscured by the hood of their cloak, but their fingers moved with the confidence of someone who had long since stopped questioning the threads in her hands.

"You've come to question fate's choice."

It wasn't a question.

Cal swallowed, jaw clenched. "Yes."

A pause. Then a soft, rasping chuckle. "Ah, the burden of love. The boy who carries the storm within him seeks to undo the only thing keeping his soul tethered."

"You know what's coming," he said. "If I lose myself on that mountain, or worse, if the bond kills her—"

"She would survive it."

Cal's breath caught.

The fateweaver murmured their hands never stopped moving, pulling threads, splicing light. "The one you love is not the one fate chose, but fate chose the one you love."

The weaver's head lifted just enough for him to see a glimmer of eyes, silver like starlight through fog. "Who do you love?"

The words slammed into him.

"I need to break the bond. I don't want her bound to my fate anymore. I want to choose."

"She did choose," the Weaver hissed, standing now, their full height imposing. Their robes whispered around them like dying leaves. "You ask to unmake what the fates themselves bound. Do you think threads so easily unraveled?"

His throat was dry. "Can it be done?"

The room fell into stillness.

"Yes."

Hope twisted in his chest, fragile and desperate.

"But not without cost."

Cal stepped forward, the magic in the cabin prickling his skin. "Name it."

The Weaver's hands rose, her fingers brushing the shimmering lines above the loom. She plucked one. A brilliant emerald-gold. Another shimmered into her palm, laced with obsidian and silver.

She pressed the two threads together. They flared, pulsed once, then twisted into a knot of fire.

"If I sever them," she said, "you will not form another."

"And the cost?"

"The thread will remain sharp in your core. Over time, it may cut others."

His stomach dropped.

"All things are connected, Calcas, you can not cut one without risking the others."

Now

The forest was too quiet.

As the last curve of the Singing Wood parted, the horses slowed, hooves muffled on the moss-laced earth. Mist clung low to the ground, and the trees, once brimming with murmurs, stood still and watchful, sentinels to something far older than roots or stone.

Ahead, nestled in the crook of two gnarled trees, was the fateweaver's cabin.

It didn't look like much, a hollow of twisted timber, hunched as if burdened by the weight of all the secrets it had swallowed. Lia shifted in her place in front of Cal, her eyes fixed on the crooked doorway.

"We're here," she said, her throat raw from disuse.

Cal dismounted slowly, wincing as pain knifed through his ribs. Even with Tadhg's magic and days of rest, his body remained a battlefield. He landed hard on the forest floor and exhaled through clenched teeth.

He turned back to help her down, offering her a hand in silence. They had ridden in general quiet for almost an entire day to get here as quickly as possible, stopping several times to rest when Lia's magic had surged painfully.

Lia reached for her sword.

Cal stopped her. "She'll know," he whispered.

"I don't care."

"She'll take it as a threat."

"She should."

He didn't argue further.

Lia hesitated. "You've been here before."

It wasn't a question.

Cal nodded once.

Her jaw tightened. "And you didn't tell me."

He swallowed hard, throat dry. "No, I didn't tell anyone until Wil last night when I suggested coming here."

Lia didn't speak for several seconds. Her breath came faster, her eyes burning holes into the cabin.

"Did you come here because of me?" she asked.

"Yes." The word sank like a stone.

Lia blinked slowly, absorbing it. The storm that passed across her face was quiet, but violent. Her throat worked once, and she looked away, hiding the betrayal behind her lashes.

"I need to know," she said quietly, almost too softly for him to hear.

Her voice cracked on the last word, and Cal's heart seized.

"I—" He faltered. "I thought I wanted it gone. It was rash and selfish."

She finally looked at him, and Gods, her eyes could undo kingdoms.

Lia's expression shifted. Not softened—but fractured. Like something inside her had cracked and hadn't quite figured out what shape it would take next.

"You tried," she said.

"Yes."

"Why didn't it work?"

"I changed my mind," Cal admitted.

"Was it after the battle?"

Cal's face scrunched. "It was before. And Lia," he stepped into her, cradling her face in his hands, "I have never regretted walking out of here."

She leaned into his palm as the door creaked open.

The Fateweaver stood inside, robed and veiled, their voice curling around them like smoke.

"You return," she said, her tone clipped. "And you bring the one whose thread you nearly unspooled."

Lia stiffened beside him.

"Come."

LITHIA

The door shut behind them with a sound that echoed with finality.

Lia stopped just inside, her breath held as if the air might shatter her.

This was not a room built of wood and magic. It was a *threshold*. Like the door to the temple in the mountains, this place was an in-between.

It reeked of fate.

Threads dangled from the ceiling. They shimmered faintly in the gloom, silver and violet and gold, some pulsing like veins. Some were limp. Some were taut. And some, when she looked at them too long, seemed to *watch her back*.

The fateweaver stood beneath them, their robe so long it pooled on the uneven floor. Their face was hidden behind a veil stitched from strands of moonlight. Their hands, pale and bird-like, twitched idly at their sides, fingers miming movement across a loom she hadn't touched yet.

Lia couldn't look away from them.

But it wasn't fear that rooted her.

Her stomach turned.

She turned to Cal slowly, her voice low and controlled, like a sword sheathed but not safe. "You came here."

He nodded.

"You tried to sever the bond."

His lips parted, no words emerging. Then, "I thought it was the right choice."

"And you didn't tell me."

"No."

The betrayal was quiet. It didn't need a scream. It pulsed through her blood like poison laced with memory. She could feel every moment of soft breath and aching glance thread itself into a knot in her throat.

The weaver finally moved.

"You are angry with him," they said simply. "As you should be."

Cal flinched.

"But you are not here for wrath," their voice no louder than snowfall. "You are here to heal threads, not sever them."

Lia's eyes narrowed.

"Fate does not deal in gifts, Mo Bhanrighit," the weaver replied. "It demands sacrifice before it gives. He had to come to me, not to win, but to *fail*. Not to sever, but to *prepare*."

Lia frowned, not understanding.

The weaver turned toward her loom, and the air changed. It became thick, slow, like time itself hesitated to flow in her presence. Threads stirred, drawn toward their hands.

"I needed him," they said, "to make you walk through that door. I needed you broken. And he, Calcas, the boy forged in regret, was the only one who could do it *right*."

Lia felt the words sink into her, cold and precise.

The weaver faced her now. "The Heart of Suviel is not shards to be picked from the ground. It is not a weapon to be wielded. It is a *song*, a memory, a grief so ancient it no longer remembers its own name. It must be *woven* into someone who has suffered, someone who has survived. It must be forged in death and blood."

Lia didn't speak.

She couldn't. The truth was crowding her lungs.

"You have gathered the pieces," the weaver continued. "You have endured much, my queen, but they remain broken because the fragments alone are not enough."

"And if I can't?" Lia asked quietly.

The weaver tilted their head. "Then Suviel dies. Slowly. Silently. And death rises in its place."

A pause. A heartbeat.

"I'm not the one who was supposed to fix this," Lia whispered. "I'm just—"

"—a soldier," the weaver finished. "A general. A queen. A girl who was told she was too much and not enough in the same breath. Yes. You are all of those things. And that is why it has to be you."

Her voice softened, almost kind.

"You are not perfect. You are *wounded*. And it is only the wounded who can carry the weight of a world, because they know what it means to *break*."

Lia lifted her chin. "Do it."

The weaver smiled. Not cruelly. But not kindly either.

She stepped back, raising her hands.

And the loom began to *sing*.

It reverberated through Lia's bones, through her blood. The threads hanging from the ceiling stirred, then *rushed* toward her, a storm of light and memory.

One wound itself around her arm, a golden thread, crackling with fire. It slid into her skin like it belonged there.

Another spiraled down her spine, cold and steady, stone. Earth. Patience and pain.

A third wrapped around her throat like a whisper. Old. Hungry.

Each thread did not ask for permission.

Each thread *knew her*.

They didn't simply touch her. They *wove her together.*

She felt herself unmade.

Dismantled.

Rebuilt.

She felt every wound she had ever suffered light up like a constellation, each one now tied to a thread that pulsed with *meaning.*

This wasn't power. It was a *memory turned weapon.*

The weaver's voice entered her mind, soft and rhythmic.

This is the pain you carried in silence. This is the song you learned with no name. This is the truth buried under duty. This is the echo of all you survived.

She wept.

Blinding white light exploded from her chest, filling the cabin and washing out her vision. The magic seared through her as it adhered to her own core and absorbed into her.

The loom quieted.

The threads dimmed.

The weaver exhaled.

LITHIA

Inside the weaver's cabin, the fire had died to embers. A hush clung to the wooden walls, thick as dust, heavy as prophecy. Cal slept curled in the crook of a chair, his body finally stilled, but his brow still furrowed with tension he couldn't shake even in dreams. Lia watched him for a long time, studying the quiet slope of his shoulders, the way one hand remained open on his thigh, reaching, even in sleep.

Her body hummed with too much magic to rest.

The heart within her had woven into her magic. She felt it in the rhythm of her pulse, in the stretch of her spine, every motion carried weight now, as though her body had grown heavier with purpose.

She slipped outside in silence.

The forest greeted her not with wind or birdsong, but with reverence. The Singing Wood bowed low with fog, the trunks of ancient trees rising around her like cathedral columns. Moonlight filtered down in fractured threads, painting the clearing in silver and pale blue.

But something else shimmered at the center.

A presence.

Not a figure at first, just a sensation. A stillness that was not emptiness. Then light gathered into form. So slowly, like watching rain become a river, stars coalesced into a crown.

She took shape in silence.

Aduna, the Goddess of Life.

She stood at the heart of the clearing, barefoot in the moss, her gown rippling with every color Lia had ever loved. The golden green of new spring leaves, the rose of sun-warmed cheeks, the bruised plum of twilight storms, the deep umber of soil after rain. Her dark skin shimmered with faint bioluminescence, like lichen lit from within. Her hair was a cascade of vines and blossoms, each petal blooming and wilting with every breath.

Lia knew her instantly.

Not because she'd ever met her. But because some part of her, the part that remembered being a child pressed to her mother's chest listening to stories of Gods and stars, had *always* known. Because the magic in her blood called to its creator.

She dropped to one knee, head bowed low.

"You don't have to kneel, daughter," Aduna said, and her voice was the first fire ever lit, the first breeze ever felt. "You bear enough weight already."

Lia stood, slowly. "You came."

"You called," Aduna replied simply. "Even if you didn't know it."

Lia stared in silence.

"I felt you," the Goddess said. "When the last thread entered your heart, Suviel itself exhaled for the first time in a century. The land knows you now. The trees, the water, the air. They have a heart again."

Her throat tightened. "I don't feel like one."

Aduna stepped closer, studying her. "Do you know what a queen is, Lithia?"

Lia shook her head.

"A queen is not a woman in a crown," Aduna said. "She is the land's memory. The mouth through which the future speaks. A queen does not rule. She *remembers.*"

The words settled deep in Lia's bones.

"I didn't want to be chosen," Lia murmured.

"No one worthy ever does," Aduna said gently.

Silence stretched between them.

Then Lia gathered the courage to ask the question burning in her chest.

"Seren means to tear the veil."

Aduna's expression darkened, the flowers in her hair drooping in sudden sorrow. "Yes. She walks the path of the unmaker now. Not because she is evil. But because she is empty."

"Can the heart stop her?"

Aduna looked at her for a long time. Then, with infinite care, said, "Not in the way you expect."

Lia's stomach dropped.

"You are the Heart now," Aduna said. "But the void is not a wound to be stitched. It is a hunger. It cannot be healed. It must be *banished*."

Her mind raced. "So...when the time comes, I'll use it to push her back."

"Yes," Aduna said. "You will cast her into the chasm. It sounds like some great ceremony, but her second death will suffice."

"But will that bring anything back?" Lia asked. "The people we lost. The land. The ones the void consumed."

Aduna stepped closer. "What the void unravels, even the Gods cannot rethread. The burned will not rise. The devoured will not return. You will end the bleeding. Not undo the loss."

Lia's voice cracked. "Then what's the point?"

The Goddess reached forward and touched her chest, just above the heart.

"This," she said. "You. The point is that something lives. That the world *remembers*. That grief births resolve instead of ruin. That which remains is *honored*."

Lia nodded slowly, bitter and reverent all at once. "You speak in riddles."

"I speak in *truths*," Aduna said. "And in one more."

She stepped back, and the clearing grew stiller than silence.

"You are the last," she said.

Lia froze. "What?"

"The final queen of Mab's magical inheritance."

The words struck with the force of a blade.

"When you die," Aduna said, "the Heart will unspool from your body and return to the land. One final blooming. One final mending. Suviel will rise again, but not through bloodlines. Through soil. Through ashes. Through *memory*."

"I'm not a vessel," Lia whispered. "I'm a seed."

The Goddess smiled.

"Exactly."

Tears blurred her vision. She didn't know if they were grief or clarity.

A long silence followed.

Then Lia swallowed hard and said, "I have a request."

Aduna looked at her, the smile not quite fading.

"Thahaos," Lia said. "He's paid enough."

Aduna tilted her head. "The gatekeeper."

"He lost his wife. He gave up his daughter. He stood alone at the mouth of

The Beneath for longer than any soul should endure. His penance is penance no longer. Let him walk free. Let him see the sky. Let him...let him *hold his daughter's hand.*"

Aduna's expression changed—gentled, softened.

"You ask not for yourself, but for another," she said. "That is what makes you worthy, Lia."

Lia blinked against fresh tears.

"When the threat has been banished to the chasm, I will visit Thahaos," Aduna said. "I believe he has more than earned his freedom in helping heal what he wrought."

Lia let out a shaking breath and pressed a hand over her heart. "Thank you."

Aduna stepped closer once more.

"I do not offer comfort," she said, "but I do offer this: when the final hour comes, you will not stand alone."

Lia raised her gaze. "Who will be with me?"

Aduna smiled.

"Everyone who ever loved you."

Then she stepped back.

And the clearing filled with wind, not cold, not harsh, but *awakening.* Flowers bloomed at Lia's feet, ephemeral and wild. For one brief moment, she heard laughter in the leaves. Then Aduna vanished.

And the Goddess was gone, and Lia stood alone again. The heart pulsed steadily in her chest. She looked up at the moon, knowing that the end was coming, and she prayed for the Suviel she would find on the other side.

CALCAS

They saw the smoke first.

Not thin columns, but thick curtains of ash, smeared across the horizon like a bruise. The Citadel should have shimmered in the light of dawn. Arachin, rising above the bay like it had for a thousand years, but now, from the edge of the Singing Wood, all they saw was smoke.

Lia sat astride her horse like a statue, stone-faced, spine taut with silence. Her knuckles were white on the reins. Behind her, the last of the trees bowed in quiet mourning. Ahead, the world bled.

Cal rode up beside her, jaw clenched. His armor bore old scratches, hastily mended. The light in his eyes—storm-light—flickered with barely restrained rage. But it was his silence that spoke volumes.

The heart inside Lia pulsed once.

Warning. Recognition.

"She's here," Lia said.

The gates below were splintered. Towers crumbled. The once-impenetrable stone lay cracked like an eggshell, and inky magic shimmered in the cracks of the stone.

"No more waiting," she said, and dismounted.

They ran the length of the bridge through the haze.

The moment their boots crossed the bridge into the outer courtyard, the veil tore.

It didn't tear like cloth. It *peeled*, like skin pulled from bone. A soundless scream ripped through the sky, and from it, the wraiths poured.

They weren't like The Hunt. They were what remained when souls were devoured and dreams unraveled. Tall as men, but warped limbs too long, eyes hollow, mouths stitched with silence. Their bodies flickered in and out of focus, as if they belonged to a different reality altogether.

And there weren't many, but they descended with viciousness.

Lia's blade was a blur, wrapped now in silver-gold fire. The heart channeled through her like a flood, guiding her movements with supernatural clarity. Her blade didn't just cut, it decimated. Every strike burned her past into her weapon, and the wraiths screamed as they dissolved into ash.

Cal fought beside her, a whirlwind of fury. He was fire and force, his morningstar glowing with flame, fists punching through dark mist and bone. Where Lia was precise, Cal was chaotic. He set the very ground ablaze, and the shrieking wraiths ignited like dry leaves.

They fought shoulder to shoulder, back to back, breath in rhythm, hearts as one.

Above them, dark shapes screamed through the sky as they fell from the battlements, Wil cutting through them as they approached. Neda stood just behind her, nocking arrow after arrow and loosing them into the oncoming deluge of the dead.

More burst from the ruined towers, some twice the size of men, dragging chains of smoke behind them like war banners. The battle grew frantic.

Lia ducked a strike and drove her blade upward, slicing a wraith from groin to skull. Black ichor sprayed. Another clawed her shoulder, she screamed and turned, severing its arm before incinerating the rest of it in a wave of blinding magic.

Cal's roar echoed across the plaza. He was surrounded now, his flames flickering as exhaustion crept in.

"Cal!" Lia shouted, and hurled a bolt of golden light into the mob, blasting several off their feet. She ran to him, cleaving down three more.

"We're not going to hold," he said between breaths, face pale.

"No," Lia said, and turned toward the steps of the ruined Citadel.

Because she was here.

Seren stood on the highest stair.

No longer wearing mortal flesh.

Her hair floated like smoke in water. Her eyes were black holes rimmed in the memory of starlight, and her body...pulsed. Like a tear in the world barely holding its shape.

Wraiths coiled around her like pets. The stone cracked beneath her feet. And when she smiled, the world grew colder.

"Hello, Lithia," she said.

Lia's boots thudded against the stone as she climbed the stairs, each step deliberate.

"You always did like making an entrance," Seren added.

Lia didn't stop. "And you always liked playing God."

Seren cocked her head. "I am no God. Gods lie. Gods *fail*. I am something cleaner. Something final."

"Don't mistake *hunger* for divinity," Lia said. "You were human once."

"I was weak once," Seren snapped. "I died screaming and begging for fate to choose differently. And no God answered..."

Lia blinked in confusion. "Thahaos answered, he gave you a purpose, a second life."

"He made me a *tool*," Seren growled, "He gave me a half-life and forced me to watch life move on without me."

And then she moved.

The first blow cracked the stairs.

Lia barely parried, her sword screeching against Seren's blade, an obsidian thing woven from magic. Sparks burst.

They clashed again—light against void. Lia's magic burned *hot*, full of memory and will and grief and hope. Seren's struck *cold*, a scream with no sound, a shadow with no source.

Each clash sent shockwaves through the Citadel.

Lia ducked a strike and drove her elbow into Seren's ribs. Her former lover staggered, then whirled and hurled a blast of magic that cracked the pillar behind them.

"You cannot win!" Seren snarled. "You *are* the last. There will be no more queens. No more Gods. No more land to bleed for. Only silence."

"I don't fight to win," Lia growled. "I fight to remember."

And she surged forward, blade flashing.

They traded blow after blow, and the world seemed to shudder with each one.

Lia was faster.

Seren was crueler.

Blood sprayed. Stone split. A chorus of shrieks rose from the remaining wraiths as they circled the tower like vultures sensing the climax.

Then—

Seren feinted left and slashed right.

The blade caught Lia across the ribs.

Pain exploded. She gasped, stumbling, falling to one knee.

Seren raised her sword, eyes wild. "It ends here."

But Lia raised her hand and caught the strike.

Light burst from her chest like a star being born.

The threads Aduna had woven into her surged to life. Memory coiled around her limbs. Every wound she'd suffered, every life she'd touched, every moment she had *survived*—it all burned within her.

The wind stilled.

Lia stood.

And for the first time, Seren stepped back.

"You don't have to be this," Lia whispered. "We all loved you once."

"I died," Seren said, voice cracking. "And no one came."

"I came," Lia said. "I'm here now."

Something flickered in Seren's eyes, pain, maybe regret, but her mouth twisted as she raised her sword again. "Too late."

Lia drove her blade through Seren's heart.

For one suspended breath, time fractured.

Seren's scream wasn't rage. It was *release*.

Her body glowed from within, cracks racing across her skin like lightning over ice. The wraiths around them shrieked, shuddered, and collapsed into dust.

Seren reached out not to strike. To *touch*.

Lia took her hand.

And the moment their fingers met—

Seren shattered.

Not in pieces, but into starlight. Light and silence and wind. She burst into a thousand fragments and vanished into the sky like a memory finally freed.

Here, above the sea, the world stretched vast and gray, and the air smelled of brine and old salt and charred cedar. Ash still drifted from the Citadel behind them like snow, soft and choking.

Lia stood at the edge of the cliffs, staring out towards the Twin Harbors.

Seren was gone.

But the land hadn't yet remembered how to breathe.

Behind her, Arachin burned in parts. Its highest towers, broken. It's the lower city, flattened in places, as if the battle had chewed straight through the foundation. Survivors picked through the rubble. Bodies were being carried out and laid beneath silk sheets. The song of the Heart had gone quiet, the land still stunned by what had passed.

She had no crown.

No soldiers flanked her. No banners flew. Just her, boots dusted with ash, blood dried along her ribs. Cal joined her, wordlessly.

He didn't stand beside her at first, not quite. He lingered just behind, like he was still gauging the shape of her. Or maybe waiting to be sure she hadn't burned out in a moment of glory.

Lia didn't turn.

"I killed her," she said softly.

"No, you didn't," Cal replied. "She was already gone."

"Maybe I killed her twice."

They both stared out at the water, where gulls wheeled above the waves and the sky tried, weakly, to remember its blue.

"I should feel something," Lia whispered. "Relief?"

Cal nodded slowly. "You feel hollow instead."

Lia's throat tightened. "I feel like there's nothing left of me."

"You still have a body," he said. "I watched it bleed."

Her lips curved, almost a smile. "You're terrible at comfort."

"I'm not trying to comfort you," he said. "I'm telling you the truth."

She finally turned.

Cal looked worse than she did. A line of bruises down his neck. A burn beneath his jaw. His armor had been stripped down to the bare essentials, his shirt torn and streaked with ash and old blood. But his eyes, Gods, his mismatched eyes held steady.

"I stayed."

Silence again, but it wasn't heavy.

She looked back toward the city. "There are so many dead."

"We'll bury them."

"There are no priestesses left."

"Then we'll learn the prayers ourselves."

Lithia

Twenty Years Later

The wind over the lowlands was warm.

It carried the scent of saltgrass and wild lilac, of fresh tilled earth and hearth smoke, of parchment and ink and beginnings. The scar where the void once leached the land had healed, though the seam remained, a pale gray line where no trees grew, like a memory the earth refused to forget. Around it, the new city had been built: Ashrun, the new capital of the Hewn Court.

Stone towers low to the ground, spread in concentric circles like ripples on water. Homes roofed in living moss. No magic wove the bricks together, only hands, mortar, patience, and stubbornness. Lanterns glowed not with conjured flames but with honest fire.

And today, the city pulsed with a quiet kind of anticipation.

Thousands had gathered: fae from the old courts, representatives of the newly allied voxis, scholars from the rebuilt Temple of the Unseen, wanderers from the southern isles, and, in greatest number, the hewn fae themselves, magicless fae, those changed by the void's severance. Their ancestors had bled power; these fae and their descendants bleed strength.

It had taken years to name themselves. Years more to stop asking the old courts for space and instead build their own.

And now, at the height of the harvest moon, they would crown their prime, formally becoming one of the courts of Suveil.

The ceremony took place atop a wide plateau ringed with carved standing stones. Old fae tradition, reborn. But the stones here had no runes. They bore no glamour, no enchantment, no stored voices of long-dead queens.

Instead, each one had been hand-chiseled with the names of the fallen.

Those who hadn't survived the voiding.

Hundreds of names.

Lia stood at the center of the ring, tall beneath the cloudless sky, draped in robes of gold and gray. Her copper hair was coiled in intricate braids bound with thread from each of the fae courts.

The sword at her hip had not been drawn in years, but she wore it still—more symbol than weapon now.

She did not need steel to command.

The people knew who she was.

High Queen of the Fae. High Queen of the Fae, Prime of Suviel, Daughter of Mab, Warden of the Old Magic. Midwife of the world that came after.

The last of her line.

The first of something new.

And beside her stood Cal, as he had every day since the battle at Arachin. Broad-shouldered and grim-eyed, though peace had softened some of the lines war had drawn. He was a reminder that even broken things could serve the world again. That grief could walk beside duty. That love, even when cracked by loss, could be chosen again and again.

The crowd quieted.

A hush spread like a tide, one body to the next, until the only sound was the wind and the low, rustling breath of anticipation.

From the path of the eastern stone, she came.

Ayla.

She moved like she belonged here. Not with the studied elegance of the old nobility, but with the firm, grounded grace of someone who had built every step of her path with the tiny hands of a thief in a fighting pit desperate to save her family.

She wore robes the color of dried blood and burnt gold. No gemstones. No metal. Just earth-dyed fabrics, a necklace of woven bone, and a mantle sewn from the banners of the first seven hewnborn clans. Her eyes were bright and clear.

Lia watched her come and felt only pride.

Not hers.

Ayla's.

A pride earned by stone laid on stone, by arguments and labor, and the long, slow work of turning grief into governance. She had seen primes rise and fall. But Ayla—Ayla had risen from a void of ash and rot, not inheritance.

At the platform's center, Ayla knelt.

The land held its breath.

Lia stepped forward, holding the circlet.

Not silver. Not gold. It had been carved from ashwood, from the first tree to grow over Seren's grave. Dark as night, smooth as glass. Its only ornament was a shard of starlight.

She lifted the circlet high.

"Ayla of the hewnborn," she said, her voice steady and bright, echoing across the stones, "you were not born to power. You did not inherit bloodlines or prophecy. But still, you rose. You led. You bound the broken. You held the line where others faltered."

Ayla bowed her head.

Lia's voice grew quieter, more intimate, though the wind carried every word.

"Do you vow to lead not with pride, but purpose? To guard not power, but people? To bear this role not as proof of worth, but as a promise to those who walk behind you?"

"I do," Ayla said.

Lia placed the circlet upon her head.

"Then rise," said the High Queen, and stepped back.

Ayla stood.

Prime of the Hewn Court.

Much later, as the stars woke and lanterns shimmered to life, Lia stood at the edge of the celebration. The music had begun, pipes and drums and handclaps. People danced. There was laughter. There was life. Thahaos spun several younglings around to the music. He smiled and bowed to her as he caught her eye before being pulled into another cackling dance.

Cal found her in the quiet.

As always.

He handed her a cup of wine.

"You didn't dance," he said.

She hummed lightly in response, sipping the sweet honey wine.

"You look older," Cal said, leaning on the rail beside her.

"I *am* older."

"Still terrifying, though."

She smiled. "That's why you married me."

He shrugged. "It helped."

They watched as Ayla danced with her advisors and her brothers in the floating lights, boots scuffing stone, arms raised. She didn't need magic to command awe.

Cal took her hand. They stood like that for a while, the two of them, in silence.

High Queen and King Consort. No throne between them.

Lia would see the story miswritten in some myth long from then as she read to the children in the Citadel and remind them how history changes depending on who's telling the story.

"And thus was the Human Court forged, not from power, but from what power left behind."

ACKNOWLEDGEMENTS

This story was not easy for me to finish, I restarted it more than once, I had more than one meltdown and almost threw the whole series away so if you made it this far...thank you. Thank you for wanting to see this story to the end. Thank you for giving it a chance. I don't know if I will ever write this type of fantasy again so thank you for growing with me as well.

Thank you to Kay for being the most supportive editor. Thank you to Vii for thinking the villain was as swoon worthy as I do! Thank you Rachel for always blowing me away with the cover art.

Thank you to EC Garret, Hillary Raymer, Whitney Dean, and Steph Blair for being such a wonderful support system. To the One More Book Club for listening to my keyboard clacks and existential crisis on a regular basis, I toast my PBJeggs to you all. Rileigh there aren't any spiders this time just for you.

Thank you Diana for always running full sprint to read a new chapter and always cheering for me as loud as possible.

Thank you Chy for pulling me off every ledge in every lifetime.

Most importantly thank you to my son and husband. I could do absolutely none of this without you and I wouldn't want to. I love you both to the moon and back endlessly. (Sorry I disappeared for like a week to finish writing I have no time management skills)

Thank you and thank you and thank you.

-Poppy

ABOUT THE AUTHOR

Poppy Roberts has always been a passionate lover of stories and has finally decided it was time to tell one of her own.

As a child she always enjoyed playing pretend, inventing stories, and immersing herself in imaginary worlds. Now, as an adult, she still gets excited about fairy rings, magical creatures, and discovering entirely new worlds. Her mother encouraged her love of reading at a young age, and Poppy's search for that magical feeling has only grown stronger over time.

www.ingramcontent.com/pod-product-compliance
Lightning Source LLC
Chambersburg PA
CBHW020250010826
48973CB00006B/1724